Summer Island Romance

Ciara Knight

Summer Island Romance
Book IV
Friendship Beach Series
Copyright ©2022 by Ciara Knight
All rights reserved.

Cover art by Yocla Cover Designs
Edited by Bev Katz Rosenbaum
Copy Edit by Jenny Rarden
Proofreading by Rachel

Reader Letter

Dear Reader,

Wow, it's difficult to believe we've reached the story of the last Friendster. I've enjoyed all the reviews, comments, and emails from readers in response to this series. It's been such a joy to revisit the sights, sounds, and smells of my youth in the shores of the Banana River and the Atlantic Ocean. The outdoor world where I've spent time climbing trees to jump off their long, sturdy branches into the ocean, crabbing, and being chased away by ducks (they can be mean when you get close to their eggs).

I hope you enjoy Wind's story. If you'd like to read more from this world, please let me know by filling out the contact form on my website at ciaraknight.com.

Enjoy escaping to Summer Island one more time!

Sincerely,
Ciara

Chapter One

HEAT, humidity, and heartache hammered Wind Lively. Heat from the sun, not to mention her not-so-pleasant summer moments. Humidity from the Florida spring showers. Heartache from the drop-dead king of sizzle, Damon Reynolds, strutting across Main Street.

What did that make Wind? The court jester?

Kat Stein, best friend and professional butt-in-ski, stopped her stroller with a squeal from little Allie. "You gonna talk to the man or stand there like a peeping Tonya all day?"

"Don't know what you mean." Wind swatted away Kat's comment and tore her gaze from the man who claimed to not want attention yet walked like he was receiving the Mr. Summer Island award.

Her pulse revved when he approached, but to her relief, he ducked into the post office, allowing her to breathe again.

"Enough. You like him. He likes you. What's the problem? Should I play like grade school and go tell him you want to marry him?"

"No!" Wind fluffed her newly colored vibrant red hair and lifted her chin. "You've got it wrong. We don't even like each other anymore. We had a minute-long relationship in high school and then a reunion moment when he came home." She huffed and puffed her cheeks out. "Did you know he accused me of being all drama and no direction? He said all I care about is attention and not what matters in life."

Kat tickled Allie's chin. Her friend had gone from corporate cougar to mesmerized mama. That baby had melted her steely gaze into softer than five-thousand-thread Egyptian cotton.

"Hey, you. Remember me?" Wind asked.

Allie smiled, sweeping Wind's bitterness away. "You know that's just gas, right?"

Kat swatted the duck hanging over Allie, then moved the stroller forward. "You know I love you the way you are and you don't have to change for anyone, right?"

"But?" Wind readied for the woman's long list of Wind's faults.

"Nothing. That's it. You need to stop trying to be someone you're not and show Damon who you really are. The vibrant, happy, make-everyone-laugh woman with a big heart."

"I'm not trying to change. Not for him, not for any man. I'm too old and too stubborn for that."

Kat tilted her head in that cross-examination way of hers. "Really? Then why did you volunteer to help clean up the beach?"

Wind stiffened.

"And offer to help pull weeds from Old Mannie's lawn?"

Wind tugged at the silk scarf tied around her neck which felt like it tightened with each breath. "I thought you said I had a good heart. What? I don't want to help my neighbor and have some town pride?"

"Big heart, yes. Helping others, yes. Getting your nails dirty in the soil and picking up smelly, icky things? No." Kat stopped again as if she couldn't take five steps without touching little Allie. "All I'm saying is be yourself. You're kind and generous and loveable, and the more you try to be someone you're not, the more people will think you're acting instead of doing."

Her words were like walking over broken shells in the soft sand—piercing but not harmful. "I get it."

Damon came out of the post office holding an envelope. He stuffed it in his pocket, then spotted them walking his way. The sun broke through the rips in the blue and white awning over his head, causing light rays to glisten on his sandy hair and reflect off his I'm-so-sexy aviators.

He waved and headed their way.

Wind's breath caught, torn between wanting to flee and frozen in place.

Kat nudged her. "Be yourself," she said out the corner of her mouth.

"Hey, I've been wanting to meet this new addition to Summer Island. I was disappointed I couldn't make the shower, but I had to go back to New York to settle some things." He slid his glasses from his face in his best *Top Gun* move and bent over the carriage. What was it about babies? They always stole the show.

Wind hated herself for resenting her six-week-old goddaughter, especially one as special as Allie. Kat slid her foot over and nudged Wind's toes.

"Hey, how's it going?" Wind mumbled.

Kat shot her a sideways eyebrow raise.

"Good. Busy with the restaurant." He stood to his impressive six-foot-one and offered that lopsided grin of his.

"Good luck with that." Wind heard the bitterness in her tone, but it was too late to retract it now.

"You don't think I'll pull this off?"

"I didn't say that. It's just that you're going up against Cassie, who's been the only restaurant in town for years. Skip's protective of her, and we all know that woman can be a challenge."

"I like a good challenge."

"Apparently not." Wind faced him with the best condescending face she could muster.

He pushed his shoulders back. "I can handle any challenge I wish to accept."

Kat nudged the stroller between them. "I, for one, am excited about your venture. We'll need a place to hold meetings with potential donors, and I'm sure you'll be offering more than deep-fried everything."

"That's right. I heard about that amazing facility you and your husband are building. Let me know if there's anything you need. One of my dear friends up north has a child with Asperger's, and they had to fight so hard to receive services." Damon put back on his sunglasses, shielding his perfect silver eyes, which made it easier to face him. "And the menu? Think five-star food with beach ease."

"That sounds perfect. You know, Wind's actually helping with the center. She's been organizing promotions, public relations, and donors for us."

"That's a perfect job for her."

"What's that supposed to mean?" Wind snipped, wanting to smack the back of his head with her Kelly Wynne tote.

He shook his head. "Don't be so sensitive. I meant it as a compliment."

Wind glowered. Damon crossed his arms over his chest.

Kat rolled her eyes. "Get a room with a view already."

"Excuse me?" Wind snapped her attention to her ex-best friend. "Never gonna happen."

Damon tipped his head as if dismissing his subjects. "I won't keep you. I'm sure you need to get to your nail appointment." He sauntered off with the air of superiority she both loved and despised about him.

Wind felt the pinch of his judgment. "How dare he."

"What? You don't have a nail appointment?"

"That's beside the point." Wind gripped the strap of her tote bag, wishing it was Damon's neck.

Kat's phone buzzed, so Wind knew she'd need to head to whatever big meeting she had next. "Sorry. Gotta run. Go enjoy getting your nails done, and don't let him get under your skin. And you might want to find a place to hide."

"I'm not going to hide from Damon."

"No." Kat pointed up the street. "Mrs. Sheffield is looking for volunteers for something again."

Wind backstepped and eyed Main Street, settling on the convenience store. "Thanks. Catch ya later." She raced inside, past the front desk. "You didn't see me," she ordered the owner, Doug Mandrick, and went to the end of the aisle.

The bell jingled over the door in warning, so she slipped deeper into the store behind one of the endcaps. A mirror in the corner showed her reflection, so she backed up and squatted.

"Whatcha doing down there?" Damon knelt by her side with a teasing smile. "You following me?"

"What? No." Wind eyed the end of the aisle, then him, his face in dangerous kissing range.

"Are you hiding from Mrs. Sheffield? Afraid she's going to ask you to do something for her?"

Wind wanted to bop him in his smug face. "I'm not scared of her, and I'm not so self-absorbed that I won't help people, despite your opinion."

"I never said—"

"I needed to get something." No way she'd give him an opportunity to pass judgment on her again.

"Urgently, I take it?"

"Yeah."

"What did you need so badly back here?"

She grabbed a box from the shelf. "This."

He laughed too loud, so she put a hand over his mouth. "Shh. What's so funny?"

His warm hand peeled her fingers from his mouth. "Contraception? A little presumptuous, aren't you?"

Heat surged up her chest, her neck, her face, sizzling her with embarrassment. "No, I..." Her words were lost along with her resolve to hate the man with the oh-so-sexy dimples and distracting banter that got under her actress-tough skin and enflamed her heart.

She regrouped and remembered his insults and accusations against her character, calling her self-serving and needing attention. The qualities that reminded him of his ex-wife. Ouch. A girl never wanted to be compared to an ex.

Wind wouldn't be treated like that. Not by any man. "There are other men in the world besides you, Mr. Narcissist."

Chapter Two

DAMON DIDN'T LIKE Wind mentioning other men. The hypocrisy of it wasn't lost on him, but that didn't mean he'd make it easy on her, so he stood up and waved to get Mrs. Sheffield's attention. He couldn't help himself when Wind looked so adorable cowering below the feminine hygiene and contraception endcap with her face matching her hair color. Narcisssit? Is that what she thought of him?

"I'm looking for Mr. Reynolds," she said to Doug. "I could've sworn I saw him come in here. I need to get his help building sets for our upcoming production."

Mrs. Sheffield's words shot past the diapers and hit Damon square in the avoidance zone. He ducked, nose-to-nose with Wind, her derisive smile plastered wide and bright across her face.

"What's wrong? Avoiding helping your neighbors in their time of need? I'd hate to think you were all talk. Hypocrite much?"

He could see she'd been waiting to sling that back in his face.

"Maybe I should get up and wave her over here." Wind blinked her faux lashes at him.

He grabbed her hand and held it tight. Big mistake. The chemistry between them had always been instant and intense, but he couldn't back away and show how much she affected him. Physical attraction, which had always been a constant between them, had never been their problem. The fact she was an attention-seeking woman who liked the spotlight as an actress hit too close to home with an attention-seeking ex-wife politician. "No. You wouldn't."

"Wouldn't I?"

He tightened his grip on her hand, willing her to listen. "I don't have time to design sets for some play. I have to get my restaurant ready to open."

She stuck out a faux-pouty plump lip. "But you know I love to put on a good show."

Did the woman have to remember every word he ever spoke and look delicious while she was doing it? "What do I have to do to buy your silence?" Damon asked, humbling himself. He'd certainly given Wind a hard time, but how could he admit it was the only way to keep his distance? A distance he needed to maintain in order to keep his hands and thoughts to himself.

"An apology and you to admit you've been judgmental and harsh."

"I only meant..."

She stood, but he tugged her back down. "Fine. I'm sorry."

"And you admit I'm not a selfish person."

"You're not selfish."

"Say it like you mean it."

"What are we, twelve?" He released her hand and sat back on his heels to give himself breathing distance from her man-trap perfume.

"Say it." She pointed over their heads.

"I'm sorry. You're not selfish."

"And I don't survive on attention alone."

"Oh, come on. Now you want me to lie?" The woman lived and thrived on being the center of everyone's world... his world. It was his ex-wife all over again.

"I'm going to call her over here." Her brows rose in challenge.

Mrs. Sheffield's footsteps tapped closer. "And Wind. I'm sure she came in here. She's going to direct the show."

Wind looked over his head at the mirror in the corner, then back to him. "All's forgiven. Let's go." She dragged him away from danger, both hunched like soldiers on the front lines facing town obligations. They shoved open the back door and fled up the alley to the end of the building, where she leaned against the brick wall laughing. "Boy, that was close."

"No joke. That woman's impossible to say no to."

"I thought the perfect Damon Reynolds gave to the poor, sacrificed himself for others, and leaped tall buildings in a sexy strut?"

"Dramatic much? I never pretended to be perfect."

"No, only pretended that you didn't think that I'm fabulous." The way she smiled—that teasing, coy, alluring way of hers—hooked him.

He sighed and closed the space between them, giving in to the flicker of hurt in her eyes. "I never meant to hurt you. Wind, you're fabulous just the way you are."

"And you take back accusing me of going to get my nails done because I had nothing better to do with my day?"

"But you had an appointment. That's what Mannie told me in the post office when he pointed at you on the street."

"Oh." Wind bowed her head.

He bent over to capture her gaze. "Just because you're not right for me doesn't mean you're not perfect for someone else." Someone else? Those two words had never tasted so bitter, but he had to say them. They would be the next World War of relationships, and he'd only narrowly escaped the divorce from his all-consuming ex-wife.

Wind toyed with the button on his shirt the way she toyed with his heart every time she entered the room. "Then why do you look at me that way?"

"What way?"

"Like you won't be able to take your next breath unless you kiss me."

Her lips parted, taunting him with the promise of escape from everything that was dark in the world. His breath caught. Wind Lively could have any man she wanted. Why did she want him? They were wrong in every way for each other. He swallowed hard and forced words from his mouth, despite his misfiring man-brain. "No. You're not the right woman for me. I divorced one like you. All about her, all the time. It's my time to do something I want with my life. I won't be pulled into a world with someone who will take over everything in my life."

"I don't want that." Wind leaned into him, her gorgeous emerald eyes capturing him and holding him so tight he thought his ribs would crack from the pressure.

"What *do* you want, Wind?" His voice came out a husky whisper.

He could give in and kiss her now and risk his heart or walk away and keep it safe forever.

The back door to a shop flew open and slammed against the wall.

Wind grabbed his arm. "Run." She took off with him in tow, her bejeweled sandal flopping off, but she didn't stop.

He turned, retrieved it, and chased after her.

They made it to the Shack, hung a left, and raced up Main Street until they reached Sunset, and then ran all the way to the strip of beach at the end of the road.

He collapsed onto a piece of driftwood, heaving, Wind by his side.

He'd been saved by the door opening. A moment of weakness could've cost him the freedom he'd worked so hard to achieve. The life he'd found—finding himself—by clawing through the political mess of his divorce to a senator with presidential aspirations. And he refused to get lost in another woman's world. And Wind lived in a big, theatrical world.

"That was close," she said between sputtered breaths.

"No kidding." He knelt down in front of her, cupping the soft skin of her calf, toned no doubt from all those years of dancing and performing on stage. He tried not to remember how her skin felt against his only months ago when they'd fallen back into each other's lives. He slid the sandal onto her foot and let go of her leg the way he'd let go of any hope they'd ever work as a couple.

"My Prince Charming." She smiled wickedly.

He swatted his hair from his eyes and plopped down on the beach by her side to watch the waves crash into the sand, the distant boats leaving the river, the birds floating in the cloudless sky, anywhere but those emerald eyes.

"Tell me something," Wind said, her voice dipping to an unnaturally serious tone.

"What's that?" He kept his gaze fixed straight ahead, ignoring the lure of her sensual voice like a siren to a sailor.

"You keep saying that I'm wrong for you because I'm too much like your ex-wife, yet you tell me that I'm unique and special and deserve the right man."

"Yes, so?"

"So, that's a contradiction. You say I'm like your ex yet I'm unique."

He chuckled. "You always knew how to call me out, didn't you?"

"Only when you're avoiding something. Like when

you didn't tell me that Rhonda asked you to go to the dance with you back in high school."

"I didn't want her to go missing one night. Let's face it. The woman is either brave or stupid to take on the infamous Friendsters. You, Kat, Trace, and Jewels ruled this town."

"Maybe, but you should've trusted me." Wind shrugged. "I didn't have to tell my three best friends everything."

He angled to face her. "Now who's not telling the truth? Do you remember when you told Trace, your ocean activist friend, about when I went spearfishing and accidentally shot a ray?"

Wind giggled that light, nothing-to-worry-about sound. "She was so angry."

"You think?" He blew out a long breath, releasing the memory from the archives. "She put up wanted posters all over the school for the Ray Killer with my picture on it."

"It was a joke."

"She hated me. And being on the wrong side of the Friendsters was never a good idea."

"You redeemed yourself, though. When you set all the frogs free from the science lab the night before the scheduled dissection, Trace removed your name from the enemy list."

He shook his head, remembering why this relationship didn't work out then and would never work out now. "That landed me in in-school suspension for two weeks and grounded for a month."

"But you earned the protection of the Friendsters after that."

"A club I never belonged to and that made my life too complicated." He wouldn't get into all the dirt of their past right now. "None of this matters. The physical attraction, the bantering, the distractions. All that matters is that I don't want you to be an enemy, but I can't have you in my life. I need to focus on my restaurant. Let's agree to keep our distance and be friendly."

Wind blinked at him, but the way the side of her mouth quirked up in that mischievous way of hers told him she hadn't listened to him.

"You didn't hear me, did you?"

"Oh, I heard you." She stood, smoothing out the front of her bright, geodesic-patterned shirt that accentuated her assets, and walked to the edge of the road. "You said you were attracted to me."

"Wait, what?" He chased after her all the way to the other end of the beach near Trace and Dustin's hotel, which he was living in for the moment. "That's what you heard?"

"It's what you said."

This woman would be the end of him if he didn't get away. "You twist everything around."

"You do that all on your own."

"As always, we're not getting anywhere with this conversation, so I'm going to head back to work."

"You sure it's safe to walk the street?" Wind put both hands on his shoulders and stood on her toes to see over his head toward his exit. Her touch made him doubt his choices, and that made him even more confident that he needed to keep a great distance from Wind and her swaying hips and full lips.

"I'm sure." He escaped her touch and rounded the corner.

Mrs. Sheffield headed straight for them, obviously on her way to the hotel to find him. "There you two are." She slid between them, put one hand in the crook of his arm and the other in Wind's, and marched forward. "Now, let's talk about how you two together will be helping with the play."

Chapter Three

WIND STOOD with the worst case of stage fright. How could she run from directing a small-town play disaster now? How could she say no? How could she prove she wasn't a selfish, narcissistic actress with no desire to help anyone but herself? Better yet, how could she give a little back to the man who'd judged her so harshly? "Of course we'll help."

"Wait, what?" Damon shrugged off Mrs. Sheffield's hold on him. He shifted between his feet, scanned the street, and then turned one foot toward his retreat.

Wind wouldn't let him go that easily. The man had forgotten how there'd be no escaping when you lived in a small seaside town surrounded by water and marshlands and bossy residents. She stepped stage left and blocked his exit from his commitment. "You know how much Damon loves to help."

He stiffened, and she knew he was searching for an

excuse. "I want to help, but I have the opening of the restaurant and everything..."

Mrs. Sheffield lifted her chin and looked down through the black-rimmed glasses perched at the end of her nose. "Of course you want to help. It's so important to the community. The community that will eat at your restaurant."

Ouch. Wind had known she'd play dirty, but that was more direct than usual.

"Understood." Damon shot Wind a sideways, you're-going-to-pay-for-this look. "And of course, Wind is excited to direct the play."

"Right, yes." She erected her spine to red-carpet posture. "What play will we be putting on? *Macbeth? West Side Story? Jesus Christ Superstar?*"

Mrs. Sheffield shrugged. "Don't know the name. Rhonda wrote it."

Wind's skin tingled as if she was facing first reviews after opening night of a new Broadway show she'd starred in. "Rhonda? What?"

"Rhonda. I heard she's taken up writing. She's even been hanging out at the Shack Bri opened recently with her husband Marek. Meet me tomorrow morning at the Shack, and we'll go over the details." Mrs. Sheffield fled like she'd dropped a grenade and ducked for cover.

She had.

Rhonda, reformed enemy to the Friendsters and the least creative person Wind knew, had written a play... One Wind would be forced to mold into something worthy while she was fighting to salvage what was left of her own career. This could be the final curtain call to her thirty years on Broadway.

"What's wrong? Not feeling so ready to give back to your community?" Damon challenged her.

Life had challenged her, and in that moment, she wanted to swat it all away.

Hot anger surged up from her gut to her face. "I've been putting up with your judgment since we reconnected. Over the last year and a half, you've accused me of caring only for myself and said that I'm flighty, attention-seeking, and so full of myself I can't see what's important around me."

"I never—"

"You've said—or at least implied—such to me, and I'm tired of it. I thought you were worth the energy and time to prove myself to you, but now I realize something. You can't possibly care about me the way I thought you did, or you wouldn't enjoy the fact that I'm being forced to direct a play that could damage my career and my name as an aspiring director and script writer in Hollywood. I've longed to make the shift from acting to being behind a camera or backstage. And if anyone catches hold that I directed a flop right now, it could be the end of my new career before it starts."

Damon looked to the sidewalk as if the deep cracks held an exit route for him. "I didn't—"

"Mean to? No, I'm sure you didn't. But maybe you should stop and think about how you're the one who is absorbed with yourself and your issues and not noticing the world around you. And don't worry. I won't be pursuing you any longer. I don't want a man who doesn't love me for who I am."

"Wind..." He stepped forward, reaching for her with that soft-eyed expression that made her feel weak in the heart.

She backed away from him and all the possibilities she once believed they'd have together. "No. You were right. We're never going to be romantically involved. But we can't be friends either. At best, we're temporary neighbors. Good day to you, Mr. Reynolds." She about-faced and marched to the beach, not stopping until she'd reached Jewels's house. Her hideout from the world the last few months.

She didn't even make it two steps inside the small living room, decorated in old-beach charm, before Houdini raced from the back room and hopped up on the table, chattering as if to announce her entrance to the house and her failed love life. That little ferret could sniff out the slightest bit of information. Sometimes Wind thought he might be the secret source for the legendary Small-Town Salty Breeze line, where all gossip flowed freely through town.

"You're back early." Jewels wiped her hands which were covered in whatever substance she now toyed with for her political art pieces.

"Yep. Decided not to get my nails done." Wind flopped onto the lumpy couch, plopped her feet up on the custom driftwood table Jewels and her late husband had made, and cuddled a pillow to her chest.

Jewels sat in the chair by her side with Houdini curled up in her lap and settled for a nap. "Damon troubles?"

Wind blinked at her. "How'd you know about that?"

A lawnmower cut on outside, stirring Houdini to raise his head. He chattered at the window but didn't bother to move. Jewels stroked his head. "Small town? Remember?"

"STBL strikes again." Wind shrugged. "Well, feel free to report that I'm no longer making a fool out of myself chasing a man I had a minute-long relationship with in high school. It ended in disaster then, and it can only end in disaster now."

"What happened?" Jewels asked, her tone calm and nonjudgmental.

Wind hugged the pillow tighter to her chest. "I deserve better than a man who judges me and pushes me away one minute then almost kisses me the next." Her lips warmed, and the image of him close to her in the alley sent a shiver of want through her.

"He always did elicit a physical response from you." Jewels leaned back and studied her as if to uncover her every thought.

"It's my body chemistry misfiring from old age."

"Stop. Weren't you the one who convinced me that I wasn't too old to find love again after Joe passed away? Weren't you the one who pushed me into dating Trevor?"

"Aren't I the one waiting for you to marry the poor sap? I mean, Kat married and has a kid, Trace is married, and you started dating Trevor before she even met Dustin. What's the holdup?"

"We're not talking about me right now." Jewels scratched Houdini's head and sighed. "But you're right. We'll discuss my situation after yours. Deal?"

Wind heard that darn stroller's wheels approaching outside. "Fine, but looks like we'll be discussing it with Kat, too."

Knock. Knock. Knock.

"Come in," Jewels called out.

Kat left the stroller outside and carried a fussing Allie into their quiet space. "Sorry. Need to change her. I'll use the back room."

Houdini bolted from Wind's lap and raced up the ramp away from the baby invading his domain.

Kat eyed Houdini sulking in the corner of the room high on his platform. "He still doesn't want to share the spotlight with the baby?"

"Nope. Not good at sharing attention." Jewels twirled her fingers in the air at Allie, and the baby momentarily stopped crying but then obviously remembered she had a damp diaper and wailed.

"Be right back." Kat scooted from the room.

"Okay, spill it. What happened this time?" Jewels asked.

Wind tossed the pillow next to her. "First, the man tries to insult me, then he tried to kiss me, then insult me, then he was sweet, and then he volunteered me to direct the town play."

"And you don't want to do it."

"Rhonda wrote the play."

Jewels's mouth dropped open. "She what?"

"She wrote the play I'm supposed to direct." Wind shoved from the couch and paced the few steps to the other side of the room. "Damon's going to do the sets for the play, and I'm supposed to direct it."

Jewels clasped her clay-crusted hands together. "What're you going to do?"

"It's not that I don't want to help the town, but my agent has my Broadway show script out on submission to producers and a sitcom for television. I spent five years writing those. There was a time when I wanted nothing more than to be on that stage nightly, but I'm too old and too tired to keep living that life."

"Why don't you give up your apartment once and for all in New York City and stay with me indefinitely?"

"No."

"Why not?"

"Because eventually, you'll be living with Trevor."

A flash of fear crossed Jewels's face.

Wind studied her long-time best friend for two seconds before she knew the truth, but she asked anyway. "What? You don't want to marry him?"

"It's not that. And stop trying to change the subject. We'll discuss me after we're done with your Damon drama."

Wind flopped back on the couch. "What drama?

There isn't going to be any because there's nothing between us."

Kat entered the room with a calm Allie in her arms.

"And there isn't going to be any play. Not one that I'm directing anyway. It's time for me to return to New York and figure out my next stage in life." Wind chuckled. "Literally."

"I thought you were going to make it work here," Kat said, sitting by Wind's side with Allie cradled in her arms.

Wind sat straight in the chair, head held high. "It's not going to work. I'm leaving as soon as possible."

"But what about the play?" Jewels asked.

"I told you, no way I'm going to do it. Nothing either of you can say will change my mind. I'll fly back and forth to visit all of you, but I won't continue living in limbo in my friend's home any longer."

"That's not good news." Kat studied Wind with an apprehensive gaze.

"What's going on? You don't hesitate to tell me what to do normally. You know something I don't."

She studied Allie's tiny fingernails as if they were created by Rembrandt. "Yes."

Wind swallowed the dryness creeping into her throat, bones, and life. "What's that?"

Kat handed Allie over to Wind, who took her sweet goddaughter without complaint, even if a baby did still feel awkward in her arms. How come babies always soothed nerves and conjured warm fuzzies?

"Now that you're holding my daughter, I know you

can't run out the door or slug me. My mother set up the play because it's part of a fundraiser she and Weston planned for the center. I wasn't the one who set it up. I didn't even know about it until Mother called me. I told them I'd get you to direct it, though."

"Why would you do that?" Wind hissed, forcing a lower tone so she didn't frighten Allie.

"Because I was at the meeting with the board of the children's center when I got the call, and I didn't know what to say. I was put on the spot. I told them we'd be hosting a fundraiser, and they were excited when mother told them that Wind Lively, the actress extraordinaire from Broadway, would be directing it. I couldn't blow the meeting."

"Why would you betray me like that?" Wind's cheeks hurt. Apparently, she was out of fake-smiling practice. It had been a long minute since she'd been on stage.

"It's a thousand dollars a plate, and when we told donors about you, we sold all the spots in hours."

"You did?" Wind couldn't help but feel flattered that her name carried that much weight. She shook it off and looked to Houdini, who tiptoed closer and sniffed the air below as if to say the baby was no longer contaminated with a messy diaper.

"Yes. Don't you see we need you? I'll do something about Damon. I'll get Weston, Trevor, Marek, and Dustin to build the sets. Just tell me you'll direct the play."

"What about Rhonda?" Wind spit out with a hiss.

Kat's eyebrow rose in question. "What about her?"

"She's the one who wrote the play," Wind screeched.

Allie made a scrunched unhappy face, so Wind quickly rested her on her shoulder and patted her behind. The baby let out a big cry then a little fuss, and then she settled.

"Oh, that. Only a formality. You have full creative control over the production. You can do rewrites. The only reason the board allowed Rhonda to write it is because her second cousin donated a hefty sum to the center."

Wind let out a long breath and struggled between her commitment—to helping her friends, the children, and Summer Island—and avoiding Damon and the mess of a script she'd have to work with. "This is going to be the end of my new career and my sanity."

Chapter Four

Dust, dirt, and disappointment filled the air of the old schoolhouse turned disaster zone that Damon hoped to someday construct into his dream restaurant. His phone buzzed, and he saw his daughter's face appear on screen. Good, Serena was always a welcomed distraction. "Hey kiddo."

"Seriously? You ran away to Bluehairville?"

He deflated and collapsed against the peeling Formica desk. "Don't let your mother put you in the middle of our drama. I know she wants me to still do the good husband thing, but we're divorced."

"She didn't ask me to call. I wish you'd come home. I know you signed the divorce papers, but once Mother is in the White House, we can all relax."

"Honey, that's when the real politics begin." He blew out a long breath, not wanting to discuss this again. "I love you, but I need to be me."

"You can be you here. I'm not going to let you fade away into the lost and forgotten. You could have your own political career. Heck, we both know you were the one who navigated Mom to success."

"A success I never wanted." He sighed, digging his nail under the Formica and chipping it away the way he wanted to chip away the past that kept following him. "Besides, I'm fulfilling a lifelong dream of opening a restaurant."

"I want you to be happy, I do, but what do you know about restaurants?"

"I worked as a chef before I met your mother and then as a food critic for years before I was sucked into the political journalism world. I know what people want."

"Then come back to New York and open one here. I'll even help with marketing and PR." Serena sighed, and he prepared for her next tactic. "Listen, there's a political storm brewing, and you'd be able to turn the narrative if you spoke to Mom and agreed to write an article about—"

"No." He knew his sweet girl only wanted to help, but he'd spent the last thirty years married and raising children, sacrificing everything for their happiness. Now they were grown and independent, and he deserved to live the life he always wanted. "I'm where I want to be. Your mother can find another reporter to cover her. Maybe when the restaurant opens, you can come stay with me. I'm renting a hotel room right now, but once I'm stable, I'm going to build a home of my own. I'll make sure your room has an excellent river or ocean view."

"Dad, I don't have time for a vacation." Serena shook her head. "Listen, I'm going to come see you soon. We can talk then. I have to run for now. Sow whatever wild oats you didn't get to when you got married way too young and then come home. I miss you."

Conversations erupted in muffled chaos on the other end of the line—a rush of activity he didn't miss. He preferred the quiet island life and didn't want the drama of the city following him here. "Just you, right?"

"Just me, Dad. Gotta run. Talk soon." Serena's call ended as abruptly as they always did. He didn't blame her. She was young and hungry for success. Pride didn't begin to describe how he felt about her, yet he wished she had more in life than career success.

Love.

That's what he wanted for her.

His chest tightened, and he rubbed his sternum. Visions of Wind and their near kiss heated his skin. An unwelcomed feeling thanks to this heat and his desire to remain single and free from anything remotely distracting in life.

Damon settled in at his makeshift desk and lawn chair that squealed in protest under his weight. He flipped through page after page of documentation, overwhelmed with the hoops and politics he'd have to jump through to get his restaurant construction completed. He'd escaped to this small seaside town to avoid big-time politics and had landed in the middle of a new kind of complication.

He rested his head in his hands, sweat dripping down

his back with the air flow blocked by the hurricane-proof cement box. The first thing he'd do is open the wall up facing the water and put in a large picture window with hurricane shutters.

His thoughts drifted to Wind and how he'd love to show her the view. They'd once enjoyed the beach, skipping class to go surfing or swimming. Those were only memories, not current reality. They didn't work then, and they wouldn't work now. She was too...too...everything.

"Hey, someone in there?" Dustin Hawk's voice called from the front doorless entry.

"Back here." Damon stood to greet the man he'd gotten to know a little since he'd been residing in the man's waterfront motel.

Dustin entered, eyeing the exposed wood beams overhead, the cement floors, and the decaying school furniture. "I see you've got your work cut out for you."

They did the obligatory man-shake, and Damon pointed to the chair across from him. "I wasn't sure you'd show."

"Why's that?" Dustin slid his fingers through his thick, wavy hair and sat down on the lawn chair at the old desk.

Damon didn't want to fall into any more drama, but he sure needed Dustin's help. "I know you've navigated all this stuff to restore your motel, but I should tell you that Wind and I had a...moment this morning. I'm not sure if you knew."

He laughed, a hearty type that made Damon feel like he'd missed something. "In this town? I heard before the disagreement ended. Don't worry. Trace already told me I needed to help you out since I'd been through this already. She said I needed a new project before I drove her nuts tinkering with anything I could find in the hotel. I'm more of a bulldozer and sledgehammer kind of guy."

Damon relaxed into his chair and pointed to the screen. "That's good to hear because I was sent to this site to read through everything, but the website refers to documents that aren't anywhere to be found."

"Ha. They're trying to see how serious you are about this project and how long you intend on staying. They want more money in the town, but there's this weird resistance to tourism. Heck, when Trevor tried to open his sailboat chartering company, he had it the worst. If it hadn't been for Jewels, he wouldn't have succeeded. Without Trace and Kat intervening, I wouldn't have a motel, so let's see if I can send some outsider help your way."

Dustin eyed the screen. "First of all, forget about the forms. Yeah, they need to be filled out and I can help with that, but there's something more important you have to do first."

"What's that?"

"Figure out what long-term resident is blocking this from happening."

Damon shook his head. "Why would anyone want to block me from opening a restaurant? There's only one other on the island."

"Ah, and there's your answer. Cassie's has been the only spot in town for a long time."

Damon rubbed the tight muscles in the back of his neck. "So you think she's been trying to thwart my renovation with all these zoning requirements?"

Dustin stood and walked around. With his hands on his hips, he faced the far wall, the one that needed a window. "No, not likely. She's not the type to do that. The woman doesn't mind healthy competition. However, there's someone else who wouldn't want to see you succeed."

"Who's that?"

Dustin turned on his heels, his rubber soles squealing against the floor. "Skip. I bet that's who's making noise."

"Why would she care about Cassie's?"

"They've known each other a long time, and if there's one thing Skip defends, it's her friends, however misguided it might be."

Damon rubbed his head, trying to rid himself of the headache that started earlier when Wind told him he was a hypocrite. She wasn't wrong.

Dustin clapped Damon on the shoulder. "Best do some recon to find out. I think we need to take a trip to the hardware store."

The big open doorway that led into town didn't look inviting. Damon would rather remain in the putrid, sauna-like old schoolhouse than take a chance on running into Wind again.

"Don't worry. We won't see her. She's at Jewels's with Kat. Trace was on her way over when I left the motel."

Damon stood and grabbed his wallet. "Can I buy you lunch? I hear there's a place called Cassie's in town."

"Sure. You can tell me why Wind's so upset so I'm prepared when I get home this afternoon. Trevor's out on a charter, but he said he'd help out, too. Wes is too busy with the baby and the opening of his facility, but Marek said to let him know what he can do."

"I don't think I've met Marek or Wes yet. I mean, I know Marek is Bri's husband and Weston is Kat's, but that's about it."

"You'll like them both. We know how the Friendsters can be, so us men need to stick together."

They walked out the door, down the gravel road along the canal to the heart of the town. Damon would've preferred something in the main section, but he liked the view of the water and the fact he'd have space to expand if things went well.

"So, what's up with you and Wind?"

Damon slid his sunglasses on so he could see past the blinding sun overhead. In New York, there were tall buildings to block the sun's rays. Here he felt like a snail crossing a desert. He liked the heat but needed to get used to the bright sun always shining. "Not much to tell really. We dated for a minute in high school. It was one of those epic-and-over kind of relationships. We both left town. I married a few years later and only returned here recently after my divorce. Wind returned a year or so ago and has been popping in and out of town. We reconnected, but after our initial reunion, I remembered we're not right for each other."

At the corner, they turned right on Main, crossed over, and headed for the hardware store.

"Why do you say that?"

Damon wasn't sure if Dustin was working recon on him for the girls or what, but the line of questioning made him feel like he was back on stage supporting his wife's career. He put on his diplomatic persona and said, "I explained to Wind that I got out of a relationship with a woman who required all the air and everyone's attention around her so she could succeed in politics. That wasn't the life for me, and I'm finally free."

"And you're worried Wind is going to take your freedom away?"

"Something like that." He shrugged. "I wanted to support my ex-wife in her dreams, but she didn't have time for a marriage. If she could've kept me as a partner she would have, but there was no love left between us."

"Understood." Damon opened the door to the hardware store and stepped inside. The old-fashioned bell overhead chimed. "Oh, one question."

"What's that?"

Dustin's grin curved into a mischievous warning. "Are you averse to marriage if it means you can open your restaurant?"

Damon stopped dead in his tracks. A nervous energy zapped through his body. "Excuse me? I don't understand."

"You will in a minute." He patted him on the back and stepped farther into the six-foot-high shelves of hardware supplies creating rows that led to the other end, where the register sat on a counter. The place had that old musty smell that permeated the older damp buildings in Florida.

"Good afternoon." Skip shuffled from behind the counter. Her short salt and pepper wisps peaked from under her hat like tiny horns. "Oh, it's the eligible Damon Reynolds. I hear you're a free man now."

Dustin shot a sideways look at Damon, then stepped aside as if retreating from the conversation.

"My daughter, Rhonda. Have you met her?"

Chapter Five

WIND SNUCK out of the house before morning coffee time in hopes of avoiding Jewels's challenging expression. The morning sun beat down with harsh, skin-spotting rays, so Wind tugged her hat down lower on her head. Not even her expensive, prescription anti-aging sunscreen could combat those UV rays.

She knew she couldn't let Kat down, but how could she work on something Rhonda wrote when she still hadn't heard back from her agent? Death before birth of her screenwriting career would be inevitable if the bigwigs caught hold of what she was doing, even if it was pro bono.

Still, Kat had promised she could do massive rewrites, and perhaps the script wasn't as bad as Wind feared, so she hung a left on Main and discovered a group congregating outside the courthouse ahead.

She crossed the street and found Wes and Dustin

handing out flyers. Trevor carried boxes from the building and dropped them next to his new buddies in crime.

"What's going on?" Wind asked.

Wes passed her a flyer. *Come to a town hall meeting Friday to hear from Damon Reynolds about his plans for a new restaurant in town. He'll speak about how this new eatery will not compete with the existing businesses and will bring in potential revenue to the town without increasing unwanted strangers to our community.*

The words evoked two emotions—dread that he'd succeed and remain in Summer Island, where she'd have to see him daily, and hope he'd stay so he could see she'd changed. She hated herself for still caring what he thought of her and she would never let him know it mattered, but for now, all she could do was focus on her own life. "Tell him good luck for me." She passed the flyer back to Wes.

"Will you attend?" Dustin asked.

"No reason to. It doesn't make a difference to me if he comes or goes." Wind almost believed her own words, but based on the way Trevor and Dustin glanced at each other, she could tell they hadn't bought her blasé attitude. "Anyhoo, gots to run."

"Wait." Dustin shifted to block her escape route. "You headed to meet Mrs. Sheffield at the Shack?"

"Yeah, why?" Wind stalled at the curb. "You heading that way?"

"I need to get these to her. Would you mind helping?" He pointed to four boxes on the ground by his side. "If you could carry one, it would really help."

Wind adjusted her sunglasses, nudged her purse higher on her shoulder, and held out her arms. "Sure."

"Great." He lifted one and put it in her arms. "Just a second."

He went to the side door of the courthouse and waved for someone inside. Out stepped Damon, dressed in slacks and a polo shirt, looking oh so handsome as always. Wind took a step back, and Dustin had to grab her arm before she stepped into the road.

"Whooa."

"Looks like the Mansters are taking a page out of the Friendsters' handbook." She shook him off and adjusted the box in her arms.

"What can I say? We learned from the best. Now show that pretty smile of yours, and you'll own him." Dustin winked. She saw what Trace found attractive in Dustin. He wasn't Wind's type but was definitely a good- and distinguished-looking man, with his dark hair dusted with a slight bit of gray. Why couldn't she fall for the nice guy who bent over backward for the woman he loved?

Damon caught sight of her, and his body stiffened.

Traver said something to Damon too quietly for Wind to hear, but it elicited a nod from Damon and he lifted the remaining boxes. "Thanks for your help." His biceps bulged against the mid-muscle cut of his sleeves.

She'd always been a sucker for a well-defined physique. "Right. Where we going?"

"To the meeting at the Shack. Drop these off and say hi to Kat and Allie for me." Wes lit up. The man had it bad.

"Sure thing." Wind threaded through the crowd and kept her eyes straight ahead, far from the distractingly delicious Damon.

He called out from behind her, his breath dusting the side of her cheek. "Delivering these together wasn't my idea, but I'm glad they orchestrated this because I'd like to apologize." He cut her off at the intersection. "Listen. I allowed my baggage to get in the way, and I may have misjudged you. Don't agree to do this play because you're trying to prove something to me. To be honest, you were right. I am a hypocrite, because I don't have the time to volunteer so I'm going to have to tell Mrs. Sheffield no."

Wind considered explaining she didn't have a way out since she needed to try to help Kat but decided to take the moral high ground instead, even if she didn't deserve to climb that hill. "News flash. I'm not doing it to make myself look good. I'm doing it to help a good cause." It wasn't a lie, just not the entire story.

"I see." He looked down at the box full of notebooks and flyers and other stuff. "Well, I'm sorry I can't help. If there was any way that I could, then I wouldn't leave you on your own."

"How you going to tell Mrs. Sheffield you're bailing?" Wind chuckled, knowing she was about to watch a whodunit comedy.

"I'm just going to tell her," Damon said, as if there wouldn't be an issue.

"Riiiight. Because she's so easy to say no to."

"I'll say no. It doesn't matter what she throws at me,

because there's no way for me to find the time to construct the sets and finish building my restaurant. I wish you all the best, though. You'll do great."

Wind adjusted the box in her arms and faced him squarely. "That's the nicest thing you've said to me in the last several months. I'll take it as a compliment."

He deflated. The ruggedly strong and powerful man in front of her looked...humble. "You're right, and I'm sorry for that. I was so busy trying to prove to you that we're not right for each other that I crossed a line. I'm not open to dating at all. I've spent too much time focusing on a relationship, and now's my time to focus on what I want." He lowered the boxes and looked over them as if to study her reaction. "I know I sound selfish, but I need boundaries in my life. It's okay if you hate me."

Wind couldn't hate him for that. She'd heard a few things about his marriage from the STBL. "I don't hate you." She brushed past him, crossed the road, and reached the steps to the Shack. Not hating and being expected to control her desire were two separate issues, and she wasn't ready to face the latter.

"Thanks. I appreciate you saying that." Damon raced up to the front door, rested the boxes on his knee, and grabbed the handle. "You know you're someone special, right?"

"We both know that. Even if you try to deny it." She strutted through the door and found Kat next to Allie's stroller, her mother—who'd surprisingly decided to stick around with her granddaughter for a while—Mrs.

Sheffield, Rhonda, and several other people around the table.

A relief that she'd not be forced to work side-by-side with a man who didn't want her like she wanted him calmed her a little. Perhaps she'd make it through this nightmare of a project unscathed after all. She strutted in and dropped the boxes on the table before eyeing Rhonda, who stood there with a smug smile.

She stood and plopped into Wind's arms bound paper the thickness of *War and Peace*.

"What's this?" Wind asked.

"My manuscript," Rhonda said with a bright-eyed gaze. "I hear we'll be co-directing."

Chapter Six

The Shack had a cool, artsy vibe with a long kitchen at the wall, different coastal-colored chairs and tables, and a jewelry display filled with ocean-inspired necklaces, bracelets, and earrings. Paintings hung along the wall with vibrant colors and signs specifying date and time of art classes.

"I'm sorry, but I don't think this is doable," Wind said in a sympathetic but unyielding tone.

Kat cleared her throat. "Actually, Rhonda, we can't spare you. You said you wanted to work PR. We'll need you to contact various reporters and bloggers. Without publicity, this entire center will fail."

Rhonda sat taller, and Wind relaxed. "Of course. I'm happy to help if you need me that badly."

Damon set the boxes down and backstepped, deciding now wasn't the time to discuss his exit from the project, but

Wind caught sight of his retreat. "Didn't you have something you wanted to say?"

A hundred reasons flashed through his head, but if he'd learned anything in politics it was to state the facts and avoid explanation, so he pushed his shoulders back and lifted his chin. "I'm afraid that I won't be able to help with the building of the sets." Gazes—judgmental, unwelcoming, I'm-going-to-put-squirrels-in-your-attic kinds of expressions —drilled into his resolve. "The restaurant has so many issues with the town zoning, and construction costs are mounting. I need to focus on shifting through all of that right now." So much for keeping the information to a minimum.

"Perfect." Kat stood and twirled her fingers at the stroller by her side. "Because we don't need you to work the sets anymore. Trace volunteered Dustin, and Trevor is going to help him."

"Great. Glad to hear it worked out." He turned to escape, but not fast enough before Kat rounded the table and blocked the door with her hands clasped in front of her.

"We need you for another purpose."

He didn't want to ask but knew he had no choice. "What?"

"Don't worry. It's more about how we can help you. We've decided to host the dinner theater at your restaurant."

Excitement, hope, and body-numbing terror all rolled through him. "I don't know when I'll get the restaurant up and running. I mean, there's a stop order for historical preservation reasons that I'm trying to fight, but who knows how long that'll take."

Mrs. Sheffield tapped her pen against the long table scattered with half-empty coffee mugs and shell decorations. "That's why you'll want to do this. We'll help push through the zoning for you since several board members of the center are also county commissioners or friends and family of them."

"What about Cassie's?" he asked.

"Her food's delightful but not appropriate for this event. We were planning on catering from Cocoa Beach, but the prices are so high and they're not willing to negotiate even for charity, so based on what we've heard about your menu plans, we think you'd be perfect."

Damon knew how this shakedown would go. He'd seen enough handshakes and under-the-table dealings supporting his ex-wife to last several lifetimes. "How long will I have to get the restaurant up and running before this big event?"

"Sixty days," Mrs. Sheffield said as if she'd given him a year.

He eyed Rhonda, Kat, several people he didn't recognize, and Wind. No one offered him any advice, only expectant gazes. Well, except for Wind, who looked like she wanted to hit him over the head with that oversized manuscript. "It'll be tight. Besides, I have the town meeting Friday."

"We have all the confidence in the world in you. As for

the town meeting, we hear that Skip is already recruiting reinforcements to push you from the agenda," Mrs. Sheffield said.

Kat nodded. "This event will give you the opportunity to have the community turn out to try your food and win them over. This will make you part of the community instead of an outsider."

"I see." And he did. There'd be no choice. He'd be hosting this fundraiser or the restaurant would never open. "How quickly will the stop order be lifted?"

"Is tomorrow morning soon enough?" asked an older lady sitting next to the stroller who he guessed was Kat's mother.

"Yes, that'll be good. Thanks." He about-faced and raced from the Shack before any more news or orders would be dropped on him.

Stress and politics, two things he'd moved here to escape, but now he found himself knee-deep in small-town political quicksand.

"I'd say you escaped with fewer wounds than I did." Wind sauntered past him, acting like the manuscript caused her to hunch over from the weight of it.

He stepped down from the porch and headed to the other side of Main, falling into step with her. "I'm not so sure. You could always skim-read that and write your own with the same premise. That should be doable. I only have sixty days to build, stock, hire personnel, create the menu, and hire a chef.

"I have a few weeks to create a show that won't cause

people to fall asleep or leave before they open their wallets."

They crossed the street, and he eyed the way to the restaurant.

"Let me ask you something?"

He stopped at the corner and faced her. "What's that?"

"Is it worth it?"

"Is what worth it?"

"The restaurant? You moving here to have something of your own, only to have it controlled by town politics?" Wind plopped the manuscript on her hip as if it were a baby.

He thought about her question for a minute, realizing she had a point. "Yes, because in the end, I'm not trying to puff up some candidate for everyone to vote for. I'm providing a place where people can come to escape and enjoy a meal. I'm building what I want instead of slaving for someone else's desires."

Wind stepped into the shade and removed her sunglasses as if to see him better. "Why's that so important to you? Providing a space for people to enjoy a meal?"

He shrugged. "I guess because the only time I felt connected to my family in the last decade was at a dinner table. Of course, all my ex-wife would talk about was her latest aspirations, but the kids would share their lives and we'd all laugh at times. It was the only time I ever felt like I had a real family."

"Food does bring people together." Wind nodded.

"Then I hope you get everything worked out. I'm sure Dustin and the other guys can help."

"I think the Florida heat is getting to me, because I think you're actually being sincere."

She slid her glasses back onto her face. "You think you know me so well. You believe that I'm not capable of human emotions and caring for others, but that's your own shortsightedness showing. Good luck." She sauntered away, her hips swaying like a pendulum, hypnotizing him.

Once she was beyond his view, he shook off the distraction and faced the truth of her words.

He'd been hiding behind his judgment of all the reasons she wasn't right for him to avoid any romantic distractions, but truth be told, he didn't want to face his own failings. No matter how much he blamed politics and his ex-wife's aspirations, it took two to make a marriage work, and he knew deep down he'd failed in his own way by giving in to her dreams and sacrificing his own. He should've fought harder for what he wanted in order to keep the marriage alive, but by the time he'd realized his mistake, the damage had been done.

Would he be capable of keeping his focus on what he wanted if he allowed a woman into his life? He'd always wanted to give a relationship his all or walk away. There had to be a way to balance it, but he hadn't figured out how. Even now, he wanted to chase after Wind and tell her how fabulous she was, despite the fact he needed to get to work.

He had to stay focused on his plan without distractions

for now. Maybe later he could open his heart again. Of course, Wind would be gone later, off to some Broadway show, and then he'd be able to breathe again. He only hoped that day would come soon and in the meantime, he'd be so busy with the restaurant he wouldn't have to see her too often.

Everything would work out in the end. He just needed to figure out a way to stop thinking about her, since she held his attention all day and in his dreams. Impossible dreams of her by his side running a restaurant in this little town. It's why he'd let her go before. She'd said it herself. She was working toward becoming a famous script or screen writer. Damon knew she'd succeed the way she'd always succeeded. She deserved the spotlight, not a small-town hideout from the world.

Chapter Seven

Wind sat on the floor of Jules's home, her back against the couch with a third of Rhonda's manuscript crumpled and tossed on the floor. Her head pounded and her eyes stung. The only thing keeping her sane was the copious amounts of coffee Kat had delivered from the Shack a few hours ago.

Jewels entered the living room, flushed from working in her art studio behind the house. "That bad?"

Houdini hopped down from the table, rolled over on the floor, and played dead.

"Yep, that about sums it up." Wind loved Houdini's drama-king ways. They understood each other.

Jewels stood in front of the air vent, turning back and forth with her arms raised. "What's it about?"

"I'm on page one hundred and fifty, and I have no idea. She didn't even format it correctly. There's a dog, and a girl, and a friend, and they go walking together along a beach and they read books. That's it. There's no goal, no motivation, and zero conflict. She's literally walking the dog." Wind collapsed back and covered her eyes with her palms. "This is a disaster. What am I going to do?"

"Trace is on her way over. Maybe she can give you some advice or bury the manuscript for you." Jewels sighed. "Could some lunch help make things better? I'd be happy to make something."

"Thanks, but Bri sent over some food for both of us. It's in the fridge, so if you want to grab it, we can eat together. I need a break."

Two knocks and the door opened to a smiling Trace. A sight Wind still had to get used to. The moody girl had turned all happily married, and it was nauseating at times. "Geesh, you trying to build a mountain out of crumpled paper or what?"

"All that's unusable." Wind crumpled up the next page and tossed it on top of the pile with a grumble.

Trace picked up a piece and unfurled it. "Where's the usable pile?"

"Doesn't exist." Wind pointed to the hundreds of unread pages still resting in a neat pile on the table. "Unless there's something in there I haven't read yet."

"I'm sorry. If it makes you feel any better, Dustin reported that Skip has sent Rhonda to Damon's restaurant a dozen times today, delivering one screw or nail at a time. He's thinking about barricading himself inside, but Dustin talked him out of it since there's no working air conditioning yet and with all the windows boarded up, there's no airflow."

Poor guy. She should go save him. No. Wouldn't happen. "Why would I care?" Wind said, eyeing the next page mocking her at the top of the stack. She hated herself for wanting a man who clearly didn't want her.

"Right. You don't care. Just like Damon claims he doesn't care. We'll go with that for now." Trace sat in the chair, and Houdini batted at a crumpled piece of paper, chasing it around the room, but gave up after a few minutes and curled into a fetal position on the table.

Wind thought about asking her what she meant but decided against it. She didn't need any more false hope where Damon was concerned, so she scanned the next page and the next one and the next one. "There's nothing here. I can't even trim this down into anything. I can't create a play with no script, and we don't have much time. Ninety days to write the script, find talent, rehearse, make costumes, lighting, and oh so much more."

"Pasta salad?" Jewels called out. "Looks like one of Bri's creations, so it should be good.

Wind tossed her red ink pen onto the driftwood coffee table. "Sure. I could use the break."

"I've got a better idea. Why don't we go for a swim? There's something I want to show you guys over by the hotel anyway." Trace's eyes lit up with mischief, not her usual look.

The mystery hooked Wind. "I'm intrigued. Let's pack that pasta salad to go. Maybe some fresh air will help inspire me." She raced to her room, put on her suit and cover-up, and then returned to the living room, ignoring the heaping pile of volunteer work waiting for her. How did she get suckered into a nonpaying gig she didn't want? Oh, right, because she'd been trying to one-up the man who didn't care about her and couldn't say no to a friend who needed her.

Trace tugged Wind's chiffon sleeve too hard, causing a tiny rip in the seam. "Hey, need your help. Trevor's got a plan, and I need to get Jewels over there," Trace whispered, eyeing their friend still fidgeting in the kitchen. "Can you get her to clean up without making it look like we need her to look better? I mean, I don't really want to take her over there with clay on her face and hands."

Wind welcomed the distraction. "I'm on it." She sauntered into the kitchen and tapped her lip, eyeing Jewels. "You know, I need a project. Something to get my mind off this."

Jewels popped the Tupperware container shut and placed it in a bag. "Oh no. I'm not going to be your next makeover."

"You'd deny a friend in need?" She batted her eyelashes, but Jewels fled the kitchen and Operation Beautify a Friend.

"I'll get cleaned up and put on my suit, and then we're heading out." Jewels backstepped away as if she feared turning her back to Wind.

"Okay, but if you come out here with your hair frizzy and clay on your skin, I'm taking over."

Jewels skittered to her room so fast Houdini didn't even catch her before she shut her door. He sulked back to the living room couch.

Wind turned to Trace in triumph.

"Nice job. Put the fear of a makeover in her. That'll motivate her." Trace held up a hand, and Wind high-fived her.

Goodness, the girl had changed from mopey hermit to outgoing socialite. Okay, maybe not that much of a change, but still. Love did strange things to people. Perhaps Wind should count herself lucky for never falling in love or marrying.

Jewels joined them with beach bag in tow, face clean and hair neatly in a bun.

"I guess I'll have to tackle Trace's look later."

She opened the door and took two large steps away. "Oh no, I've already secured my man."

They both looked to Jewels.

"What?"

Houdini shot out the door, letting them know he was tired of waiting.

"Stay in the tunnels," Jewels called after him, but that little rodent somehow would find a way out if he wanted to. How many times had Trever and Jewels fixed the tunnels, only to find another opening between the pipes and the wire mesh?

"He listens to you about as well as I do," Wind teased.

"You're not wrong." She closed the door, and the three of them headed to the beach. "We should call Kat."

"She's already there. It was her idea for me to come get you." Trace stalled at the edge of the old souvenir shop that had a rental sign out front. Wind didn't understand why Jewels hadn't moved her workshop into that space where there was air conditioning, but perhaps it held too many memories of Joe. Wind couldn't pretend to know what it was like to lose a husband.

"So, how are you and Trevor doing? Any ring talk?" Trace asked.

Jewels slowed her pace, and her eyes shot wide. "No. Why?"

"What's wrong? Don't want to marry him?" Wind asked. "You know, if you don't marry him, we'll end up two old ferret ladies who have nothing to do but take over the SIBL."

"Would that be so bad?" Jewels asked, her gaze steady on the ground ahead.

Wind snagged her by the elbow and pulled her to a stop. "Okay, spill it."

"What?" Trace asked.

"I get the impression our girl here doesn't want to marry Trevor, the man she's in love with, and I want to know why."

"I didn't say I didn't want to marry him."

"Then what is it?" Trace asked.

Jewels sighed. "I don't know. It's just everything is so good and exciting and fresh. What if...oh, it sounds silly."

"You end up in a stale relationship where you care about each other but the passion is gone?" Trace asked, an uncharacteristically insightful relationship question that caused Wind to arch a brow at her.

Trace shrugged. "I might have been talking to Kat, and she might have pointed that out."

Jewels toed a loose pebble on the path. "Perhaps. Don't get me wrong. I loved Joe, deeply. We had an amazing marriage."

"We know. But you've had that, and now you want something different." Wind rubbed her arm. "Have you talked to Trevor about this?"

"No. I mean, everything is so perfect. Why do we have to mess with it?" Jewels asked, the lines around her eyes deepening with worry.

"Perhaps it won't make your relationship stale but make it better." Wind offered, hopping to show her beloved friend that it was okay to move on and not hold on to the past.

"Do you really think that's possible?" Jewels looked to them both.

Wind grabbed the beach bag from her and slung it over her shoulder. "Well, you did fall for Trevor naked at first sight. Maybe you're just a horny old woman looking to get some."

"That was an accident and you know it. How was I supposed to know he was going to use the outdoor shower?" Jewels laughed, lightening the mood.

If Wind didn't know better, she'd swear her sweet, motherly Jewels had discovered the world of lust along with love. Wind shook her head. Since when had all her friends changed so much? Why couldn't things remain how they were?

Obviously Trace was satisfied with their conversation, because she quickened her pace. "Come on. You don't want to miss this."

They hurried to the end of the street, hung a right, and walked along the docks behind the hotel toward the woods that led to Trace's place.

"What's going on?" Jewels asked when they entered the woods.

"Not much farther." Trace led them through the woods until they reached the edge, where a smiling but pacing Trevor waited.

"Hi." He took a deep breath and took both of Jewels's hands in his. "I know you've been hesitant to move forward with our relationship, and I'm not going to push you into marriage or anything, but I think I've found a compromise. Follow me. I have a surprise for you."

He led her out of the woods to a cleared area, where orange ribbon in long lines was tied to wooden stakes in the ground.

Trace tugged Wind back. "I think we should give them some room."

"What's he doing? Is he really not proposing to her? Coward." Wind chuckled.

"Nope, not doing that today. Showing her the home he's going to build for them, though." Trace nudged Wind toward the road. Apparently they weren't taking the wooded route again, which meant they'd have to pass by Damon's restaurant on the way back.

Wind stopped dead at the edge of the asphalt. "Wait. What are you doing now?"

"I'm not doing anything." Trace's raised eyebrows told a different story.

"Yeah, right. I think I'll take the long way around." She turned toward Main, but shouting drew her attention to the restaurant.

"Get out! No!" Damon's voice echoed with fear from inside the old school building.

"Sounds like Damon." Trace took off, ready to help, and Wind found herself following before she thought better of it.

They reached the doorway to see a hissing, spitting alligator. Damon poked at it with a two-by-four, only making it angrier.

The alligator snapped at him, but he couldn't get around the beast to get out.

"Don't be a hero. Get up on the counter," Wind yelled.

Trace pulled out her cell phone. "I'll call animal control. Wind's right. Climb up where it can't get you."

"No, I can shoo it out."

"Before or after it snaps that two-by-four and your femur bone in half?" Trace's words lit a fire under Damon's feet, and he leapt up on the counter, where he squatted in the corner, still wielding the long wood beam.

Trace dialed and walked away to make her call.

"Come on. Facing people and zoning and backhand

deals is one thing, but siccing an alligator on me? That's a new level of evil."

"You think the town council put the alligator in your place to chase you away?" Wind asked, keeping her distance far enough that she wouldn't be the gator's next meal.

Trace returned with a nod. "Should be here in ten to fifteen."

"Would you put it past these crazy town folk? I mean, I've dealt with my share of political tactics, but this has to be the worst."

"They wouldn't do that," Wind announced but then glanced at Trace. "Would they?"

"No. Of course not." Trace shrugged. "Don't think."

He swatted his hair away from his brow, losing focus, and the gator grabbed ahold of the wood and yanked it from his hands.

"We need to block the gator in there." Trace spun and then stopped, pointing at wood against the outside wall. "Here, help me with this plywood."

Lying it on its side so it would cover the double door, it only stood four feet high. "Think that'll hold it? I thought a gator climbed Mr. Mannie's fence once and he took care of it old-school style. Or is that a legend he made up?"

Trace shook her head. "Don't know. Just improvising here."

Wind nudged closer, her shins pressed to the board resting against the doorframe, but the gator turned on them, and she backed away. "Shouldn't we do something to help him?"

"Like what? You want to wrestle the thing?" Trace stepped back. "Don't worry. Animal control is on its way. He won't have to stay there much longer, and he's safe up there. Not like the gator's going to be able to climb up there to eat him."

Wind wanted to help, but Trace was right, so she hollered into the room, "Don't worry. Help is on the way."

They each grabbed an end of the plywood and slid it to block the door, then another piece, and then another, and finally one more. "You think that'll hold it in there?" Wind asked.

Trace shrugged. "Not sure."

Damon shifted, trying to get farther from the gator scratching at the cabinet below him. "All the years I lived here growing up, I only saw gators in the marsh areas. What's it doing here? If I find out someone led that thing in here, I'm gonna—"

Wind forced a calm to her voice she didn't feel inside. "No one would do that. Now listen. Just stay where you are, and you'll be fine."

"How do you know that?" Damon looked genuinely scared, not a look Wind had ever seen on him before. Of course, who wouldn't be frightened by an angry gator?

"Because Trace, remember? Animal activist extraordinaire? She says the gator can't climb up there, and she's already called animal control."

"Okay, good to know." He leaned his head back against the wall and took in a deep breath.

Trace leaned in. "I don't know anything about gators."

"Shh." Wind shooed her away. "Listen, the worst thing you can do is panic and end up falling off that counter. Talk to me. Tell me about the first thing that pops into your head that makes you smile."

Damon lowered his chin and locked gazes with her across the room with a hissing gator between them. "You."

Chapter Eight

DAMON EYED the alligator with its mouth open, jacked teeth in need of major dental work, ready to chomp him. Adrenaline flooded him, and his hands shook. He looked to Wind, who stood at the opening of the door. "Get out of here. Those boards won't hold the gator if it charges you."

Wind crossed her arms over her chest and popped that distracting hip out. "I dare that beast to come near me. I'll hit it over the head with my beach bag." She lifted a bag from where she'd dropped it to the ground nearby.

The gator clawed harder at the cabinets, scarring the wood with deep ridges. Better the furniture than his skin. He feared the counter wouldn't hold him much longer. His breath stung his lungs with each fast and furious intake of air.

"Look at me. I'm the one who makes you happy." She winked.

Oh right, he had blurted that out, hadn't he? Darn

gator was wrecking not only his place but his brain. But he didn't take it back because it was true. She did make him smile each time she entered a room. The way she spoke, the way she moved, the way she smiled all beguiled him. "Any sign of animal control?"

Trace lifted her phone in the air. "I'll call again." She slipped from sight.

Wind clapped her hands. "Hey, you. Mr. Gator. Over here."

The gator didn't even turn its head.

Cracks sounded beneath him. He peered down to spot the molding splintering. "They better get here quick, or I'm going to be gator food."

He shifted his weight, and the cabinet collapsed a few inches beneath him. His pulse pounded harder than the gator's jaw clamped down on the molding sticking out at the base corner, turning the shrapnel to dust.

Wind's eyes shot wide. She reached into her bag and popped open a container. "Let's hope he likes pasta salad." She closed her eyes and appeared to say a silent prayer.

"Wait. What are you doing?" Damon asked. "Get out of here. I don't want you hurt." He didn't. The idea of anything happening to Wind scared him more than those hungry, demon-yellow eyes looking up at him.

"When I toss this over there, you run for it. Got it?"

"That's a stupid plan."

"You got another idea?"

He shook his head. The gator turned and looked behind him toward Wind. She gasped and tossed the container to the far end of the room, pasta salad splattering across the floor. The gator hissed and moved faster than Damon wanted to know it could toward his snack.

"Now." Wind waved at him. "Go."

Damon watched the gator's tail swipe back and forth as it skittered to the pasta. Damon leapt from the counter, stumbled over an upturned chair, and slid across the room.

The gator turned to look at him. Wind's hands reached over the plywood and yanked him until he moved. He tumbled over the barricade, sending it sliding across the rocky road.

She kept tugging at him.

"Okay, I'm okay."

"Yeah, well, we're not going to be in a minute." Wind pointed over his head.

Damon glanced over his shoulder and spotted the gator scratching at the floor, leaving gashes in the cement. It spit and scurried at them. "Go, go. Go!" He found his footing, grabbed Wind by the hand, and raced toward Trace. "Get out of there!"

Trace ran for the hotel. Wind scampered up a tree, so he followed her. They managed to climb to an old platform in a massive oak tree.

She collapsed by his side, panting. He took her hand, needing to touch her to make sure she was really okay. He peered down and spotted the gator on the sidewalk out front of the restaurant. A shaggy stray dog taunted it from up the street with barks and growls.

"Get out of there," Damon shouted and waved his free

hand. He held his breath until the dog took off and the gator decided chasing live creatures wasn't as easy as slithering back inside the restaurant for his easy pasta snack.

With the gator out of sight, adrenaline seeped from his pores, and he collapsed by Wind's side, temple to temple with her. "You're insane, you know that? Why would you risk your life like that?"

Between gasps, she said, "Don't let it go to your head. I'd do it for anyone."

Damon rolled onto his side and noticed blood on her cheek. A searing energy shot through his every nerve. "Are you alright?" He brushed the blood from her skin with his thumb to find a tiny scratch.

"Fine. Just a branch got me."

He hovered over her, realizing the woman he'd dismissed as superficial and frivolous was brave and selfless. She deserved better than he'd treated her. "I'm sorry."

"For what? You didn't invite the gator to the party," Wind teased. Always using humor to block her real feelings.

"For my fear and doubt of my own ability control my feelings, which caused me to behave as if you're not good enough for me...when I think it's the opposite." He pressed a kiss to her flushed cheek. His pulse quickened, and he thought he could lose himself in her beautiful, wide eyes.

"What was that for?" she asked, her chest rising and falling in a way that would demand any man's attention.

"For saving my life." He leaned down and kissed her other cheek. The warmth of her body and the softness of her skin reminded him how much passion always consumed them before he could think, but his fear didn't stop him. How could it, when he'd just faced much worse? "And that's an apology for not treating you like the goddess you are."

She cupped his cheek and lifted her head to plant a kiss at the edge of his mouth.

"What was that for?" he asked.

"For not dying on me."

His head spun with possibilities. He couldn't let go of her. He could take her in his arms and taste her sweet lips. Lose himself in the fun and exciting world of Wind Lively, the best place in the world to escape and enjoy.

Her thumb brushed over his lips, leaving heat behind. She leaned up to kiss him.

His chest tightened, his body craving what she offered, but his brain screamed to stop. "No." He leaned away, but when he saw the pain in her eyes, it crushed him.

She shoved from his arms and leaned over the platform. "Animal control arrived. Looks like the gator's making a run for it," she said in a shaky voice, one laced with passion and disappointment.

Disappointment he'd caused after she'd just risked her life to save his. He was a selfish prick for behaving this way. He needed to make this right. "Wind?"

No response, not even a glance. She climbed down and was gone.

Damon collapsed, breathless, wanting, and confused.

WIND DIDN'T STOP until she reached Jewels's house. Panting, sweat dripping from her temples, she stood hunched over in the living room, eyeing a judgmental Houdini sitting on the back of the chair. She trembled with want and hate. How could caring for someone be so difficult? "One word, that's all he gave me."

Trace shut the door behind her. Obviously she'd kept in shape better, because she wasn't even breathing hard. "One word? Who? Damon? What did he say?"

She stood straight, rubbing her Botox-tight forehead. "That man drew me into his arms with a look that would make a trucker on I-75 blush. And he kissed me."

"Kissed you?"

Wind paced, ignoring Houdini swatting at her to stop. "Yeah, on the cheek, but it was more than a sweet gesture. There was hunger in his eyes. He...he...drew me in and then..."

Silence filled the room, and Wind knew Trace struggled with what to say next so she continued ranting. "Then I kissed him back, and he responded. Ohhhhh, did he respond, but then. Then he rejected me. Me, Wind Lively. The one men usually claw over each other for even a chance glance of me. He said, 'no.' That was it. One word."

"Ha," Trace said before she settled on the couch and put her feet up like they were about to watch some romantic comedy with popcorn. But the only thing popping was Wind's temper.

"Ha? That's what you have to say? What, you don't think men still find me attractive?"

"Nope. Not what I'm saying at all." Trace chuckled. "You know how fabulous you are. Don't you dare doubt yourself. I'm only saying you like him because he challenges you. For years, you've never had to work to get a man to kiss your feet, but now, Damon doesn't fall at your jeweled sandals so easily."

"No. That's not it. I mean, why would any girl in her right mind want a man to play with her emotions like this?" Right mind. Maybe her menopausal brain made her mad.

"There's your answer," Trace said, leaning back with her hands behind her head.

"What?"

"You've never been in your right mind."

Wind picked up a pillow and threw it at her. "You stink at girl talk. You know that, right?"

Trace tossed the pillow back at her. "If you wanted to be placated, you'd speak to Jewels. You want the truth, I'm your girl."

Houdini climbed to the upper platform and chattered as if to scold them for playing in the house.

"From now on, Houdini's going to be the only man in my life."

Houdini lifted his head like he was happy to take the job.

"Come on. You know you're not done with Damon. Not yet. You've been challenged, and you'd never back down from that." Trace plopped her feet on the floor. "The girl who was told she would never make it as an actress but became a Broadway sensation? Nope. The Wind I know would never run away."

"I'm not running away," Wind snapped.

"Think about it, then. The man keeps spouting how he doesn't want to get involved because of giving himself to his ex for so many years, yet he keeps pulling you closer to him each time he sees you. That man's confused. Maybe you can make him see the truth."

"And what's the truth?"

"You two are in love."

A smack of shock zipped over her skin. "Love? Are you insane? I'm a fifty-year-old woman who's never truly loved anyone but herself."

Trace tilted her head. "You love us, and you are gaga over Allie."

"That's different. None of you are men." Wind's anger drained and her legs went weak, so she sat on the itchy, fabric-covered chair. Houdini ran down the platform and plopped into her lap, snuggling into her.

"Listen, you had no freedom growing up. Your parents were so strict you couldn't breathe, and you had so many siblings you were lost in the crowd. No wonder you ran away the minute you could."

"I didn't run away. I just never belonged in my family. All my gazillion siblings were so much like my parents. If my mother wasn't so devoutly religious, I'd think I might have been related to the mailman."

"You've always kept your faith. You just don't tell everyone about it. I know you still have your Bible and cross from when you were confirmed." Trace never let her escape the truth. It was one of the things she loved about her friend.

Wind shrugged. "I loved my parents, God rest their souls. They just never understood me. I'd never been able to sit still long enough to eat a meal, let alone study for a career in accounting or insurance."

"Listen, you're who you were meant to be, and even your mother admitted God made you special."

A tug at Wind's heart reminded her that despite their differences, she missed her parents. They'd passed only a few years ago, so the wound still felt fresh.

"Don't be in such a hurry with Damon. Be a partner in this venture, a friend. Keep your relationship platonic and your hands to yourself. We both know you're the bomb and he's the detonator. Together you'll explode at any moment."

"You sure you're not the writer?" Wind asked, chuckling at her analogy.

The wheels of the stroller squealed, announcing Kat's arrival.

"Not a word to Kat, 'k? I don't want to deal with another meddling friend right now."

"I'm not the girl-talk type, remember? Just promise me you won't run from this and you'll give some time to getting to know each other beyond the physical part of your relationship."

"Okay, Mom." Wind rolled her eyes. "I liked you better bitter and unattached."

"No, you didn't. You just want what I have and you won't admit it to yourself."

"Hogwash."

The door opened, and Kat carried in Allie. Wind held up her arms to take her goddaughter, needing a cuddle.

Kat obliged, sending Houdini into the corner to pout. "You two okay? I heard about the gator incident."

"Yep. Escaped mostly unscathed. Only Wind returned with a wound."

"What? I'm fine." Wind narrowed her gaze at Trace.

Trace pointed to her cheek. "Just a flesh wound, so all's good."

"Right, my cheek."

Trace grinned. "What did you think I meant? Hurt anywhere else? Like here, maybe?" She pointed to her heart.

"How's Jewels?" Wind asked while patting Allie's butt and bouncing her.

"Jewels is on her way back. She looks like she's been hit with a shock gun. From what I understand, she didn't say yes or no to Trevor. She kept the conversation on design and what the house would look like but never about living with him."

"Not a shocker. Jewels could never live with a man without marrying him."

They both looked at Wind as if she'd said the most profound thing ever.

"You're right." Trace sat forward. "So, we've been going about this all wrong. We need to get her to realize she wants to get married instead of trying to ease her into it by living with Trevor. What were we thinking?"

"I should've known you morons would try to interfere and muck everything up." Wind kissed Allie's cheek and received a smile that brightened her day. "I'm the one who brings people together. You amateurs need to step aside."

Trace shot her a you've-got-your-own-issues-to-work-out glower. But Wind needed a distraction.

Kat eyed the stack of wasted paper Rhonda called a manuscript. "How's it going?"

"I'm on it. No worries," Wind lied.

"It's trash and she can't work with it," Trace announced then shot from the couch. "Got to run help Dustin with something."

"Coward," Wind shouted after her as Trace raced out the door, slamming it behind her and startling poor Allie, who stuck a pouty lip out. Wind cuddled her close and stroked her back.

"So it's that bad?"

"Bad? Remember that 3D movie we tried to watch in the '80s but we all fell asleep in the theater?"

"Yeah... That bad?" Kat asked.

"A thousand times worse." Wind shook her head. "I don't know what I can do to fix this, but I'm still trying. Don't worry. I won't let you down."

Kat let out a long sigh. "I was worried about that. Can't you take a few main points and use them to rewrite it?"

"Sure, if I can find a few points." Wind picked up a sheet, glanced down, and saw a paragraph-long description of how a character looked at a flower, so she crumpled it and threw it down.

Allie fussed, so Kat took her and walked around bouncing her. "I have an idea. We're having an open house for parents and kids at the center. You should come. Maybe seeing what you're working for will spark your creativity. These kids are a true inspiration."

Wind shrugged.

"Let me rephrase that. I need you to come to the open house in two weeks to meet some of the people because they're coming to see the legendary Wind Lively."

She closed her eyes. "Great. Are they ready to meet a washed-up Broadway star who can't snag a part anymore, let alone a man?"

Chapter Nine

THE NEXT MORNING, Damon trudged down to the restaurant, willing himself to forget the dreams he'd been enjoying all night. Fantasies of a red-haired spitfire and her lips.

He hammered away his frustrations but couldn't shake his thoughts, so he found himself resting his head against the wall to take a breath.

A whimper sounded outside, so he tossed his tool onto the pile and went to see where the noise had come from. When he opened his temporary, keep-out-the-alligator wooden door with a hole cut out for air, he caught a glimpse of the shaggy dog he'd seen the day before. The furry mutt with stripes down the front of his face and thick but stringy hair took off to the corner, where he'd stood his ground against an alligator.

"Come here, boy. I won't hurt you. I think I owe you one."

The mutt barked twice, then took off.

"Great. Even you don't want to hang out with me today," Damon sighed, feeling the weight of loneliness creeping in. He'd wanted quiet and to be far away from the crowds of politicians, but it was depressingly vacant in his world.

Maybe a dog would be good company. Perhaps he could earn its trust. After all, he should repay the dog for distracting the killer gator while he and Wind had made their great escape.

FOR THREE DAYS, he'd arrive and begin work, only to hear a whimper outside and then run out, but only in enough time to catch a glimpse of the dog's tail before it rounded the corner at the end of the road.

On the fourth morning, Damon left a bowl of water and some food he'd picked up from the store. When he left that afternoon, the bowls were empty.

On the fifth morning, a bark sounded, and when he opened the door, the little mutt stood on his hind legs with his paws in the air.

"Hungry?"

The dog cried and sat on all fours. Damon squatted and scratched the coarse hair. "I always wanted a dog," he murmured aloud. He could never keep a pet while married because of his ex's travel schedule, but he could now. "You need a bath if you're going to stay."

The mutt dropped and rested his face on his front paws with a whimper.

"Sorry. It's the price for being fed. I can't have a flea-infested mangy dog at my restaurant."

He grabbed the dog shampoo, flea comb, and collar from the bag of supplies he'd purchased yesterday and took the little gray critter around back to the hose. "What should I call you?"

Woof.

Damon turned on the water and hosed the poor creature down. He looked like a rat, but he didn't want to call his furry friend a rodent. "Hmm... Houdini is taken."

He smoothed back the fur from his eyes and thought he looked like a rodent but something cuter. "You have unique stripes and little legs. How about Badger?"

The dog barked his reply.

"Okay, Badger it is. I only have a few rules. One, you don't beg at the table. Two, you don't sleep in bed with me, and three, you never steal people food."

THE NEXT DAY, he chased Badger down when he stole his ham sandwich. A week later, he woke to the little monster in his bed, which he thought would make him feel less lonely and keep the Wind dreams away, but he wasn't that lucky.

After two weeks, Damon worked from before dawn until late night. He'd break long enough to walk, feed, and pet Badger. He'd managed to keep to himself except a quick trip here or there for food at odd hours of the day. Work kept his hands and mind busy, mostly. On occasion, attention slipped from his work and he found himself remembering Wind's soft skin, the way her eyes lit up when he touched her cheek. That moment on the platform in the tree haunted him. One glance at her lips had caused his body to ignite.

His hammer missed the nail and smashed his hand. "Ouch!" He sucked on his throbbing thumb for a moment and sat back on his heels. The ache under his nailbed didn't even begin to match the ache in his soul.

Grrrrrr.

"It's okay, boy. Go back to sleep. Just me being stupid."

The clock that leaned against the wall, still needing to be hung, struck midnight, so he tossed his hammer into the toolbox and walked the short distance to the hotel carrying Badger like a baby in his arms.

Like every other night, he collapsed onto the bed, expecting exhaustion to win, but instead he closed his eyes with his mind and body remaining alert. Alert to the fact he had a ton of work to do before the opening, alert to the fact that he owed some small-town politicians for forcing permits through. Alert that no matter how long he'd made it without seeing Wind, her image was still etched in his mind. He tossed and turned until his alarm went off at five.

Sluggish and unsettled, he shuffled back to the restaurant, grumbling and mumbling to himself. "We don't belong together. We're too different. I won't sacrifice my dream for her." He'd already done that, and he wouldn't do it again.

Woof.

"Thanks for the support, buddy." He settled Badger in the corner and went to work.

Contractors flooded in and out as the restaurant began to take shape. Since the building had been constructed in a time when quality counted, the bones were good. After the contractors finished fixing some plumbing issues and rewiring the electrical, the place was ready for surface work.

In the late afternoon, he sat with Badger by his side, feeding him bits of his sandwich.

Grrrrr. Grrrrr. Woof!

"What is it, boy?"

Badger raced to the door and snarled and jumped.

Dustin entered and eyed the snapping dog. "You live. Guess Trace is right and you don't like us." He laughed then eyed Badger, "Who's that?"

"Badger. Don't mind him. He's mostly harmless. All bark and no bite, but don't tell any gators that." Damon wanted to explain but he didn't have the words for why he'd been avoiding everyone so he went with simple. "Tell Trace no hate, just been working overtime trying to finish this place.

Dustin knelt down and scratched Badger's head. "So you're the little one that woke up Mrs. Thompson this morning."

Damon froze. "Oh, no. I never thought to ask. Is it okay

if he stays with me in the hotel? I de-flead him, and I took him to the vet for vaccinations yesterday."

"Sure, not a problem as long as he doesn't keep our guests up at night." Dustin patted Badger's head. "You'll be good, right?"

Woof.

"I'm here to help rebuild your cabinets." He spotted the one Damon had caved in when attempting to escape the gator. "Man, look at the scratches in this wood. That might have been a little gator, but he could've diced and sliced you into bite-sized pieces."

"Don't remind me." He cut a board and held it up for Dustin to use the nail gun to secure it in place.

He eyed the doorway to make sure the place was still secure.

"Don't worry. I don't think a gator can get through those iron doors."

Damon stood and stretched the kinks from his back. "Installed those this morning. Kind of went overboard on that, but with hurricanes and skin-shredding gators, I think it's worth it. Besides, it fits the décor I was going for, and since I can open the windows in the center of the doors, it'll allow extra airflow."

The morning air brought a cool ocean breeze. He eyed the large picture window to see the sun disappearing overhead, only a sliver remaining at the top of the glass.

"It's coming along." Damon removed his gloves and tossed them on the large table in the center of the room cluttered with tools.

"Still need paint on the walls, the tables and chairs brought in and staged, the appliances installed, and some other minor cosmetic things, but for the most part, my vision of eclectic Mediterranean beachside décor is taking shape."

"I feel like I'm beside the ocean on a Greek island or something. It really is an escape to a foreign place yet right here in Summer Island."

"Thanks. The exterior'll take longer since I'm waiting on a permit to build the deck, the landscaper to send me a quote, and the electrician to wire the fans and lights outside. I want the place to feel homey, luxurious, and casual all at the same time."

"You've thought this through well."

"I've been thinking about it for twenty years." He opened the back double doors to where the porch would be constructed, only to find a drop-off into shell-covered gray sand. "People could walk in from the beach and enjoy sitting on the back deck but enjoy a fine meal, while the formal dining room will be a place for people to get dressed up and have a nice date."

"Hey, mind if I come in?" Wes called through the wrought iron on the front door windows.

"Of course not." Damon wiped his hands on a rag and greeted him in the center of the space. "What brings you here?"

Badger trotted over and sniffed Wes, who sneezed and took a step away.

"Wow, he likes you. He usually barks at everyone."

"Dogs always come around me. I swear it's because they know I'm allergic and want to torture me." Wes chuckled.

"Sorry, man. Didn't know. Badger, corner."

Badger lowered his head and sulked back to his bed.

Wes sniffled and dabbed at his eyes with his sleeve. "Came because I need a favor. Can you attend a function this evening? It's at the center to meet some of the donors. They're curious about your restaurant, so I think it'll be a good opportunity for you. I know you're really busy, but you'll get me out of a jam. Kat told me to invite you over a week ago, and with everything going on, I forgot."

Damon scanned the room and thought about the idea of being around people again. No, not people. Person. Wind. He had to face her and conquer his desire if he ever hoped to be an active member of this town. "I can probably make that work, but only for an hour or two. I've got lots of work to do, and Badger there has never been left alone."

"Great." Wes backed to the door. "Got to run. Baby duty."

"I remember those days. Good luck, man," Damon said.

Dustin brushed off his work pants and headed for the door. "I promised Trace I'd get to the leak in room three. Sorry to abandon you."

"No worries. I'm gonna finish this up then head back for a shower and a nap."

Damon sanded and stained and sweated until he thought exhaustion would keep him in check at the event.

After a quick shower, shave, and choking himself with a tie, he made his way to the center.

A skirt fluttered into the back door of the building, and his pulse quickened. Great, an unconfirmed Wind sighting and he'd already lost his senses. "Get it together, man."

A rap on the window drew him from his chastisement at himself.

"Always talk to yourself?" Wind stood with painted lips and perfect hips.

He peeled his fingers from the steering wheel and stepped from the truck. "You look nice tonight."

She did. The dress dusted her hips and kissed her waist.

"Thanks. I know." She winked and snagged his arm. "Come on. I think we're required to actually enter the building in order to count as being here. Based on your timid expression and oooh-so strained biceps"—she gave his upper arm a squeeze—"I'm thinking you want to be here as much as I do. So let's get it over with."

He didn't say anything as he trailed behind her like she held him on a short leash. His body trembled at her closeness. The same way she'd always stirred him inside. Not even his ex-wife had such control over him with her feminine wiles. He forced long, cleansing, breaths of sea breeze–filled air into his lungs.

He opened the door and thought about what excuse he could make to abandon her the minute they stepped inside, but she fled from his reach two steps later.

"Wow, this is marvelous." She spun in the center of the

atrium, drawing everyone's attention. She was a magnet, and despite him claiming to be her polar opposite, he couldn't keep his darn eyes off her.

Kat held out a drink to Damon. "I'd tell you to take a picture, but I wouldn't want to spout cliché when you're a walking one already."

He took a swig and wished it was something stronger, but considering it was a facility for children, he'd make do with the punch. "What're you talking about?" He couldn't look at the attorney stare he knew she'd be showing.

"Please. Boy loves girl, boy denies girl, boy remains miserable until girl fixes him. Walking cliché."

"I don't need fixing, and I'm not in love, and I'm not alone." He tsked and scanned the area for the nearest escape.

"Not alone?" A hint of irritation sounded in her voice. "Oh, wait. You mean the dog. Right, Wes came home sneezing and red-eyed." She chuckled.

"I'm so sorry. I didn't know he was allergic."

"Don't worry about it. He's fine. Interesting you're trying to fill the void in your life left by keeping Wind away with someone or something else. Funny... That's what Wind is doing, too."

"With whom?" he asked, but it was too late.

Kat sauntered off to join Wind in the center of the atrium, snagged her arm, and tugged her down some side hallway.

He stepped past the front desk area, through the atrium, into a waiting area filled with slides, balls, swings, and other strange contraptions. He spotted Wes waving him over to the far wall, where he stood discussing something with a person who seemed to be one of the donors.

Good. Maybe he could find out what Kat meant about Wind filling her void with someone or something else.

"Let me introduce you to our restaurateur, Damon Reynolds. He's working hard to get his place ready for our special fundraiser."

Damon shook the man's hand, disappointed he wouldn't get the chance to ask Wes anything right now. "Nice to meet you."

"Mr. Drander," the man said.

Wes pointed to the bumpy bubble seat and the swing. "Mr. Drander donated this sensory playground for our children to enjoy while they're waiting to see a practitioner."

"A sensory playground?" Damon asked but immediately wished he'd kept his mouth shut in fear he'd come across as being insensitive.

"Yes. Many kids are told they have behavioral issues because they're unable to sit still. Bringing them into a waiting room can agitate some children. Imagine feeling like you're on a rollercoaster all the time when you sit still and the only thing to relieve that feeling is movement. Then you're told to sit for twenty minutes and pay attention."

"I don't think I could do that," Damon admitted.

"Exactly." Wes pointed toward the atrium. "Let me show you both some of our therapy rooms. We have children in there now working on a special thank-you project for our donors."

They followed Wes through the atrium and down the hall Wind and Kat had taken, which was painted an ocean color with a mural of coral and sea life. Damon's breath quickened at the sound of Wind's voice.

Wes entered a code on a pad next to the door. "Some of our kids are flight risks, so we keep the doors locked. However, there's a safety lever inside to disengage in case of a fire."

The room smelled of rubber, fresh paint, and peppermint. "This is one of our therapy areas."

In the center of the room, on a circular rug, Wind sat on her knees playing with trucks with three boys. They were mesmerized by her, crawling into her lap and even messing up her hair, a sight Damon never thought he'd see in his entire life, but it was perfect. *She* was perfect.

Four little girls sat at a table painting with brushes, while one little girl was using her hands. Damon concentrated on the little girls and moved closer to them to discover the paint smelled of peppermint.

"What do you think of our spaces?" Wes asked.

Wind laughed, a hearty, happy harmony that demanded Damon's attention. "Beautiful."

Chapter Ten

WIND HELD Allie while Kat escorted the bigwigs out of the New Blessings Center. The little bundle in her arms was like a sunrise on a clear morning, pure and perfect. The baby's hair smelled fresh and clean, her breathing calm and relaxing.

"You'd make a good mother."

Damon's words shattered her moment of peace. He strutted into the heart of the play area and lifted an abandoned truck from the pile of overturned vehicles on the carpet that made it look like a twelve-car pile-up on I-4. Little boys were always full of life and action.

"Nope. Took care of that years ago. I was never meant to be a mother."

Damon tossed the vehicle into a bin and looked up at her with that sexy tilt of his head that made him look like he was posing for a perfect picture on the red carpet.

She snuggled Allie up to her neck and rotated back

and forth, enjoying the innocent snuggle that could keep her attention anywhere but Damon's strong arms that offered protection and power and passion. "I raised too many brothers and sisters for me to ever want my own."

"I can understand that. You did fill your maternal well to the brim before the age of fifteen." He snickered. "Remember the time when little Joey followed us to the beach and snapped a picture of you in your bikini with my hand on your back?"

"Oh, did I get it. Mom thought I'd boarded the express train bound for Sin and Scandalous." Wind set a sleeping and bubble-blowing Allie into the carriage.

"I didn't see you for weeks."

"That's because I was on my knees every afternoon after school begging for forgiveness and promising never to stray from the righteous path again. And in no way would I ever see the virgin reaper Damon Reynolds again."

"Until the day after you were let out of the house again." He winked. "The day you proposed we run away together, far from your family, to live an exciting and adventurous life beyond this little town."

"That's when I frightened you off." She sighed, poking out her lip that she knew always drew him in for a kiss.

"No."

He stood and joined her near the stroller, stealing all the air from her lungs. She fought to take another breath, one that would help calm her racing heart.

"It's the day I realized two things. One, I was your

hope of escape, and two, that once you got out of here, you wouldn't want me anymore."

She turned, finding herself face to face, breath to breath with the man she couldn't escape feeling inexplicably drawn to even after all these years. "You should've told me instead of shutting me out."

"I was a kid. Communication wasn't my strongest quality. Besides, you would've convinced me to leave with you."

"You left Summer Island but with a different woman." Her voice cracked under the weight of the truth. "You were willing to leave for her."

His calloused palm cupped her cheek, and she surrendered to the gentle yet rugged connection. She'd missed him. Two long weeks they'd been apart, and she'd promised herself the distance would help her get over her longing for the man who'd haunted her all these years. It didn't work.

"That was after I studied to be a chef and traveled, doing food blog work. It wasn't a decision, more of a gradual change in my life. One that I resented later."

Wind dared to catch his gaze and saw the pain. Pain of his marriage failing. She knew him well enough to realize he carried that feeling with him. The man had never liked to fail at anything in life, not then and not now. She knew that's why he had to see this restaurant through. "I get it now."

He stepped closer, his hand slipping to the nape of her neck. "You do?"

"Yes. You need to do this restaurant because you never achieved your young-adult life's dream. It's the only thing left unfinished in your life, and you've never handled leaving something unfinished. You would work into all hours of the night to complete a paper that was due, or you'd run a ridiculous marathon because you said you would even when you sprained your ankle." She blinked up at him, trying to remain connected to her thoughts and not to the idea of feeling his lips against hers one more time. "You've carried this idea of a restaurant all this time. Go. Make it happen. You know you have to."

"But what about us being together in this town? I'm confused when you're with me, and I'm miserable when I don't see you."

That had always been their problem, unable to be near each other without being together. "It's why I left," she mumbled.

"What?"

She shook her head to clear the haze. "You've always been like the ring in the *Hobbit*. Something I had to have but never could keep. I left to put distance between us. Our attraction is powerful and undeniable, but you have something to finish. I won't get in your way, and I need to figure out what's next for me."

"There's a problem. I left one other thing unfinished."

"What's that?"

"You."

She knew if they plunged into the pool of desire, they'd drown in their differences, so she mustered all the strength she could manage and slid his hand free to take a step away. A step away from the storm brewing that would only end in a state of emergency. No. If there would ever be a *them*, she had to let there be a her and a him for now.

"I see." He backed away, his gaze plummeting to the floor with disappointment.

"Damon, I won't go through you pulling me in to only push me away again. Go do what you need to, and then let me know what you decide. Until then, I'm going to get to work on what's next for me."

With only a nod, he about-faced and raced from the room, nearly knocking an approaching Kat out of the way at the door.

"Did you see the way Damon looked at you? Whoooa, I felt the temp in the room rise to smoldering."

"Stop. Not gonna happen." Wind sighed. Lord knew she'd tried to break through his fifty-foot retaining wall of emotions. "I need to get home and get back to work. That script isn't going to rewrite itself."

As if realizing she was tip-toeing on a mine field, Kat backpedaled and took the turn to non-romance conversation. "Still haven't figured it out yet?" She placed a container of toys on the shelf and eyed the room.

"No. And I'm running out of time. Rehearsals start in a few days."

Apparently approving the cleanliness of the area, Kat switched off the lights and opened the door for Wind to push the stroller through to the hallway. "Did you get any more out of the story?"

"Nope. Still just a girl not fitting in and a dog."

Kat clicked the door closed behind them. "You realize that's Rhonda's story, right?"

Wind waited outside the front door for Kat to lock it before she relinquished control of the stroller. "The thought had crossed my mind. The story is as uneventful as her life has been."

Kat shook her head. "That was mean."

"Not trying to be rude. It's a compliment. A life without conflict is a good life to live, but it doesn't make for a good story that people will want to watch. You need drama or love or murder or something. I can't have a little girl walk a dog across the stage over and over again."

Wes waited at the car. He lifted Allie with a father's tender touch and tucked her into her car seat. Wind blew a kiss to her goddaughter.

"Did the kids inspire you? This place give you any material to work with?"

Wind shrugged but noticed the worry lines on Kat's face deepened. "Maybe. Don't worry. I'll figure it out."

"I know you will." Kat hugged her, and they parted ways, which meant Wind needed to finally sit down and write something. Something that included a girl and a dog.

When she reached Jewels's place, she was still out with Trevor, so Wind fed Houdini and made her way to the desk in her room, where she sat and stared at the computer screen.

Houdini rolled a ball in with his nose to her feet then

crawled up to the table and flopped down, placing a paw on her hand as if to tell her everything would be okay.

"You're a special one, Houdini. I don't know how you always know when someone needs you." A jolt of realization shot through Wind, and inspiration took hold. "Houdini, you're a genius."

He sat up as if to take a bow.

"That's it. A special dog for a special girl. I can show the gifts of the children and how their huge hearts are a gift to all of us."

She tapped her nails against the computer keys for a few moments, contemplating how to structure the story. The inciting incident, the major plot points, the climax. Ideas tumbled over her, and characters competed for a place in her story until she settled on the ones she wanted. Her fingers tapped away for hours. She'd never written so fast.

The front door opened, and Houdini skittered out to greet Jewels like he always did when she arrived home, but Wind didn't stop. She kept typing away well into the early morning hours.

HER BACK between her shoulder blades throbbed and her eyes burned, but it wasn't until twilight that she collapsed onto the bed to catch a few hours of sleep. She dreamed of a little girl and her dog. A great journey to help someone who didn't understand her and a cranky old man who said he hated dogs and children.

She awoke seeing the remaining scenes vividly, so she pounded out the rest of the script. It had been a long time since she'd felt the rush like she had early in her career when she'd step on stage in front of a packed house.

A spark ignited within her, and for the first time since her final performance on Broadway had received scathing reviews, she felt confident and ready to face the highly critical world. First, she wanted to print it out and mark it up herself to make sure it was worthy, so she left it to print while she showered and got ready to face the world.

Maybe things would turn around for her. Certainly, she had a talent for writing. She'd reworked several off-Broadway scripts that went on to do well. Perhaps her agent had finally heard back from the bigwigs about her submission.

With renewed hope, she called her agent, but it went to voice mail. No surprise. It was still early. She'd try again in an hour or so. For now, she needed coffee, the stronger the better. And she needed to get out of her borrowed bedroom, so she slid her manuscript into an envelope and headed to the Shack for a strong cup of brew.

The ocean breeze felt invigorating, the walk got her old joints moving and feeling young again, and the aroma of honeysuckle growing along the fence line outside of the Shack made her smile.

Wind hopped up the front steps and entered the creative space Bri had offered their sweet little town.

Between this and the swanky new restaurant, Wind didn't feel like Summer Island was lacking in culture as much anymore. Perhaps their little town would finally blossom into something great. Then again, maybe it had always been amazing and Wind hadn't seen it before. The quiet definitely suited her more now than when she was young. With age came certain changes in a person.

"Good morning!" Marek, Bri's oh-so-young-and-handsome husband waved her inside to the counter. "What'll it be?"

Tabitha, Marek's daughter and now Bri's, held up a cup. "I'm in training, so give me something challenging."

Wind smiled. "Tell you what. I need something strong and not too sweet. Light, but nothing too frou-frou. Surprise me."

"That's easy." Tabitha snagged a cup and went to work.

Marek pointed to the case full of delicious treats. "Can I get you something to eat?"

"No. Since I stopped working, my middle has started growing. I think I need to start taking morning walks or something." She plopped the envelope down on the counter.

"What's that?" Marek asked.

"A script. A good one, I hope." Wind held her head high.

Marek nodded. "For the play here in town?"

"That's the one."

"Good for you."

Wind eyed Tabitha, who was working hard on her beverage. "Looks like you have a reason to be proud, too."

"I do."

Tabitha finished and slid a cup of something foamy toward Wind. "Give it a taste. Don't like it, I'll make something else on the house."

"I like her confidence." Wind took a small sip, not sure what to expect. Her eyes opened at the bitter yet creamy goodness. "Perfect."

"I did a double shot of espresso, so you shouldn't have trouble staying awake for a long time."

"You better be paying your new employee well. You don't want to lose this one."

Marek chuckled and pointed to the display of sparkly earrings, necklaces, and bracelets at the front. "She needs to pay me. I think she can pay for college herself based on what she's made off her beach jewelry. She's got an online shop now and everything thanks to Bri."

Wind's phone buzzed, so she checked it to discover her agent's name. "Sorry. Gotta take this." She swiveled her stool and walked past the couple sitting along the end of the counter as she answered.

"Hi. How's it going?"

Sandra's hoarse and overworked voice came with an I've-got-bad-news quality. "Hi, Wendy."

"Oh no. You don't call me Wendy unless it's bad news. Spill it."

A long breath sounded like a hurricane-force gale through the phone. "Afraid your play is a dud. No one wants it. But I've got a great audition for you. It's a sure thing. You just have to show up. The production is off-Broadway, but it's already being labeled as the next masterpiece."

Wind deflated. "What did they say about the script?"

"Oh hon, let's just get back to what you do best, performing. I know I can get you back on Broadway. You're too good. You're the amazing Wind Lively."

Wind rubbed her aching knee that felt the years of performing on a hardwood stage. She knew she didn't have it in her anymore to show up every night with a smile to face the people who'd decided she was washed up and too old to be a star. Her career had been amazing, but she knew when to exit stage right with dignity. And that time was now. "What didn't they like?"

Silence.

Tapping.

Throat clearing.

"Fine. I'll tell you, but I'm not going to hold back because you need to see once and for all where you belong —on stage, not writing for it. They said it had no spark, no interest factor. It was a script like the thousands of other scripts left in a slush pile over the years."

"Ouch." Wind returned to her seat and collapsed onto the stool. "Any specific notes?"

Sandra paused before speaking. "Take the audition in New York."

"Audition..." Wind sighed and eyed the manuscript in front of her. Maybe it would be good enough for the small-town play at least. Not to mention she'd felt a purpose in her life being a part of the center, something she hadn't felt in forever. She couldn't walk away and leave them without a writer and director. That wouldn't be right for those children. "I'll think about it." She hung up before her agent could nudge her into something she didn't want to do but might have no choice but to accept.

"Leaving for New York?" Damon's voice cut through her like a Ginsu knife. He stood a few steps away, holding the leash attached to his new companion.

She turned to face him, her lip trembling. Her emotions surged faster than a hot flash under the noon sun. He really believed that was the only place in the world she belonged. It was why he kept rejecting her, and maybe her agent was right. Maybe off-Broadway was all she had left in this aging body. "I'll stay for the play, but then you're right. I'm not good at anything but performing on a stage. I thrive on attention and need it twenty-four-seven. I'm nothing better than a diva." Her words scorched her throat and burned her pride, but what did it matter? She could admit when she was wrong. "You were right all along. I'll never be good enough for you or anyone else in real life. I'm only good at pretending."

Chapter Eleven

DAMON HELD tight to Badger's leash to keep himself from pulling Wind into his arms and holding her to rid her of whatever pain haunted her.

"I'll make some Puppy Whip," Tabitha said and went to work behind the counter.

Damon sat on the stool next to Wind. She turned to face him, but not with her usual vivacious personality. Her eyes were dull and full of doubt. Doubt in herself. The vibrant, confident woman had faded. Had he done that? "What's this all about? Where's my firecracker, bombshell of a woman I know?"

"She's in New York where she belongs." She drank a few gulps of coffee, keeping her gaze locked on the counter.

He needed to take a loop around instead of a straight approach to the truth. Wind was like a wild cat. If you backed her into a corner, she'd strike and run. "What's that?" He pointed to an envelope resting on the counter.

Wind sighed. "Nothing really. A sad attempt at fixing Rhonda's script for the town play."

"Great. I knew you were struggling with that." Damon longed to draw out that happy, attention-stealing woman who made him feel alive every time she walked into a room. "You're great at many things. Those kids last night..." He tucked her soft, fire-red hair behind her ear in hopes she'd look at him.

She blinked several times as if to hold back tears. "What good it'll do?" she grumbled under her breath. "I best head to Kat's and deliver this to her." She plopped some cash down on the counter. "Thanks. It was delicious."

Bri waved at her, and Marek poked his head out from a back room. "See you soon."

Bri handed over a small cup of foam. "For Badger."

He looked between the cup and Wind.

"Go. It's on the house. Come back for a drink later."

"Thanks." He gave Badger a whiff, and he obediently followed him out the door, where he caught up with Wind. "I'll go with you. I need to speak with Wes."

She stopped on the sidewalk out front. "For a guy who thinks I'm nothing more than a distraction, you sure do keep showing up."

"I didn't say you were a distraction." He shielded his eyes from the blinding sunlight. "I told you how fabulous you are, and I meant it."

"Was that before or after you almost kissed me but then rejected me?" She held the envelope tight to her chest. "It doesn't matter. Now isn't the time to chat about anything. I said my piece last night."

"Apparently not all of it." Leave it to Wind to call him out. "That was a mistake."

"Trying to kiss me or not kissing me?"

His head spun. "I-I don't know. You're the most attractive, interesting, beautiful, confusing woman I know."

"But...?" She took a step closer, and he wanted to abandon everything and chase her to New York City. Worse, he wanted her to stay but knew she didn't belong here. She was already talking about needing to return.

"I want you more than I've ever wanted anyone in my life, but I can't have you. You were right. I need to build this restaurant. See a lifelong dream come to fruition. But after that... I mean, I know your life's in New York and mine is here, but..."

"Right, my life's in New York." She looked to her sparkly shoes, and a shadow crossed her expression before she forced a smile and pushed her shoulders back. "Like I said. I have to go."

"Wait, what happened? I can see it. You're upset." He snagged her by the elbow. "What's wrong? What can I do to help?"

She didn't look at him, only at the sidewalk ahead. "It's time to stop playing games and face reality. It's time to stop being scared."

"What reality?"

"Nothing." She shook her head and marched away, leaving him to try to guess what she meant.

Badger whined and shook his head. Damon squatted and gave him the cup of foam, which apparently was a huge dog treat. He didn't stop until every last dot was licked clean, except for a bit on his nose.

"What am I going to do, boy?"

Badger barked.

"You're right. I shouldn't back down." Damon pushed up his sleeves and walked to catch up with Wind to make her tell him what was eating her up inside, but Skip poked her head outside the hardware shop.

"Your order on those fancy knobs are in."

He wanted to stop Wind and confess...confess what? What would he say? He wanted her, but it was wrong. Maybe his ex-wife was right, Wind was so attractive because she was forbidden dragon fruit. A beautiful, sweet, and different style that was rare.

"Hello?" Skip waved her hand in front of his face.

"Right, thanks." He abandoned his pursuit for now so he could think through what he really wanted. Wind was right. The games had to stop, which meant he needed to think before speaking to her again, so he followed Skip inside.

"That rat's not allowed in here," Skip shouted.

Badger whimpered and backstepped away.

"Can't leave him outside."

"No worries. I'll send Rhonda over later with them."

Damon thought about abandoning his furry friend

outside, but no way he'd take that chance, so he'd apparently be seeing Rhonda again later. He bolted from the store, irked at Skip's treatment of his new best friend.

"Don't worry. You and I will stick together."

Damon walked back to the restaurant, where Badger collapsed on his bed in the corner.

Dogs were easy. He knew exactly what Badger wanted. He was loyal, and he'd always be here when Damon arrived home. He'd never have to worry he wasn't enough for him as long as he fed Badger and gave him water and love. Wind never made sense.

He sat down on the floor and rubbed Badger's ears. Damon's phone buzzed, so he checked it to discover a message from his ex-wife, demanding he help with a campaign speech. He shut off his phone, not wanting to be bothered with anything else related to his previous life, and worked on his business. The one he could control where no one else could order him around.

Was that it? He'd been telling himself that it was about how he'd sacrificed himself for so many years for his ex-wife and he wouldn't be stupid enough to do that again, but had he missed something? Was he too scared to give Wind a chance because he knew he could never keep her? Would a summer romance be so bad?

No. He was working hard on the restaurant. His dream. She'd gotten it wrong. That wasn't it. He only wanted to allow her to leave because he never wanted to trap her the way he'd been trapped for so long. He wanted her to pursue her dreams, not sacrifice for his.

Damon worked on staining a table until his shoulders ached and Badger growled.

Knock. Knock. Knock.

Badger barked and ran for the door.

"Hush, it's fine. Gators don't knock." He sat back on his heels, hoping he could figure out a reason to usher Rhonda out quickly. "Come in."

Dustin entered with his tool belt. "Heard you had an eventful day. SIBL states you were arguing with Wind. Then got the call about her showing up at Kat's upset."

Damon let out a lungful of frustration. "Got any good news for me?"

"Thought I'd save you a visit and bring these." Dustin held up the bag of knobs.

"Thank you. That's some relief." Damon shoved his brush in the bucket and fell back against the wall. "I didn't mean to upset her. I actually was trying to be there for her, but it backfired."

"Wasn't about you." Dustin eyed the paint and abandoned his tool belt for a paint brush. "Turns out her script was rejected. Agent said she needs to return to the New York stage where she belongs."

"One rejection and she wants to give up on writing scripts?" Damon rubbed his aching back and sat forward. "I'd think that a rejection would only make her more determined."

"I think it usually would, but this time not so much. Not since she had a flop on Broadway and the critics slaughtered her for being too old to play a sexy heroine."

"Ouch." Damon's gut clenched tight. "Guess that sent her for a spin."

"You could say that. She dropped off the script for the town play but told Kat she needed to get Rhonda to work on hers, that it would probably be better than what she wrote."

"That really doesn't sound like Wind." Damon eyed the wall and the rust-colored paint. It wasn't the right color. He'd prefer something lighter, more fun. more... Wind. "What did Kat say?"

"Nothing. Didn't get the chance before Wind raced back to Jewels's, who talked her into staying in Summer Island a few more days."

"Is there anything I can do?" Damon asked.

"Wes sent me over to ask you if you could try to talk to her."

"Me? I think I'd be the last person she'd want to speak to right now."

"Maybe so, but according to Kat, you have a way of stirring her up and lighting a fire under her."

"More like her lighting me on fire." Damon chuckled. "Let me ask... Is Kat pressuring her to stay here because that's what she wants or because Wind wants it?"

Dustin eyed the appliances waiting to be installed, the chandelier on the floor waiting to be hung. "According to the Friendsters, Wind wants to move from the stage to writing and producing. Says she's tired and doesn't feel the joy anymore when she's performing."

"Because of one critic?" He'd spent so much time

urging her to return to New York and the career she loved that he never stopped to think she might actually want to remain in Summer Island. He needed to ask her and give her a chance to tell him what she wanted.

"No. Jewels thinks that watching all her friends recently settle down made her want more out of life than a lonely living in New York away from those she cares about most." Dustin eyed him as if to tell him he was the reason, but that wasn't it. Her friends had always been everything to her.

"I feel a little responsible for her decision to leave. I'll talk to her. Not that she'll listen."

Dustin leaned against the far wall, crossing his arms over his chest. "Tell me something."

"About what?"

"Did you really come back here for this restaurant or another chance with Wind?"

Chapter Twelve

Wind hoped to hide from the world, even if it was on a twin bed in white-painted, wood-paneled room with stars pasted to the ceiling, the faint odor of Clearasil and Aqua Net probably still stuck to the walls and floor.

Jewels peered in and shook her head. "You still not going to face anything?"

"I'm busy." Wind flipped a page of an old magazine she'd found in a box in the closet.

Jewels chuckled and sat on the edge of the bed. "I'm thinking you might want something more enlightening than *Teen Beat* since it's out of publication. Johnny Depp is no longer a teenage heartthrob, and Kirk Cameron is no longer starring in *Growing Pains*."

"I don't know. I still think Johnny Boy is hot in a bad pirate man kind of way."

"What about Damon? You think he's hot."

"Yeah, in an I'm-never-going-to-accept-you kind of

way." Wind slapped the magazine shut on *Alyssa Milano's Secrets Revealed* article.

"What keeps you two from pulling the trigger on romance? You've been dancing around each other for months."

"What keeps you from pulling the trigger on marriage to Trevor?" Wind shot back.

Jewels turned the magazine so it faced her and tapped the cover. "Did you ever notice there were only a few women on the front of these magazines?"

"Now you sound like Trace." Wind eyed the shiny paper. "Now that you mention it, though, no."

Jewels tapped the cover again. "I remember when I wanted to be the first woman in space, you wanted to be the first lead female in an action movie, Trace wanted to save the world, and Kat wanted to conquer it."

Wind fell back with her head resting on her pillow to look up at the ceiling. The darkening sky from an incoming storm matched her mood. "Yeah, well, childish dreams seldom come true."

"Not the way we might have imagined it, but still. Well, okay, not me since Sally Ride beat me to the job, but Kat took on the world in the courtroom, and Trace fought for sea life. I had a great life raising Bri, and you... You were a star. No one thought a little girl from some small town in Florida would ever become the infamous Wind Lively."

"Maybe so, but that time has passed." She rubbed her aching hip and knew her body couldn't continue in the type of roles she'd tried so hard to play. "Guess I'll be doing bit theater in some musty dive for the rest of my days."

Jewels bounced on the bed like they were ten. "Shut up and stop. This isn't you."

"I haven't felt like me for a while." She flicked her chipped nails at Jewels. "Leave me to wallow a while longer, and then I'll pack to return to New York. My agent wants me back to audition." She blew out an indignant breath. "Yep, I'm auditioning for an off-Broadway production."

"Don't do it." Jewels grabbed her hand and scooted closer, knocking the cover of their teen heartthrobs to the tile floor. "Listen, I know you may not even admit it to yourself, but I see it. You don't want to go. You think you don't have a place here because you didn't end up with your hero, but screw him."

"Wow, those are some powerful words coming from Mama Jewels. Do you kiss your daughter with that mouth?"

Jewels swatted her. "I'm serious. Why do you need a man? You have us."

Wind thought about it for a moment, but it didn't matter if it was on stage or in life. As much as it hurt to admit it, Damon was right. She had to be the star. And she'd only be the sidekick in their group of happily ever afters. "I appreciate that Jewels, hon. I do."

Jewels opened her mouth to spit out some more harsh words, but Wind wouldn't do this. She flung her legs over the bed. "But I'm the great Wind Lively. I'm not going to spend my golden years hiding from the world because of a failed show. I made it to the top once. I'll make it again. Maybe I don't perform as a lead young woman. Maybe I create a new path, one for women like me. Maybe I don't dance, but I can still sing, act, dazzle an audience."

Wind moved jazz hands in front of Jewels's face, provoking a smile.

"That's the Wind Lively I know." Jewels stood and yanked her into a rib-crushing hug. "I want you to be happy, but secretly I want you here. Don't give up on the script because of one rejection." She stepped away, keeping hold of her shoulders and locking the determined, motherly, you've-got-this-girl gaze. "You're Wind Lively, and you can do anything."

"Amen, sista." Kat entered the room. Apparently, without the stroller she could make stealthy entrances. "Are you done with your pity party? Because we have work to do."

She, eyed *Teen Beat* on the floor then pulled a manila envelope from her briefcase and dropped it on the bed. "The board approved it. Every member."

Wind sat on the bed and ran her fingers over the soft package of hope. "They did? Wait, there's no way. Not all the members read it in one night."

"Oh, but they did." Kat did her courtroom spin and march, coming alive as if she were about to drop a bomb of evidence on an unsuspecting courtroom. "You see, I read the first line and knew this isn't just *small-town play* material... This is *movie production* material." She tapped her lip and did a spin on her heels, crossing back towards the door. "I emailed the entire board with a dare. Read the first page, and if you can stop, then we'll find another playwright."

"That was bold." Jewels shook her head, obviously not approving of Kat's bully tactics.

"And they read it in one night?"

Kat stopped, popped her hip out, and looked down at her like a witness taking the stand. "Do you not know how brilliant that is? I laughed, I cried—"

"Still suffering from pregnancy hormones?" Wind teased, knowing the Kat she knew never cried unless she was pregnant.

"I'll put this in a vocabulary you'll understand." Kat smiled, a real, I-own-this-argument kind of grin. "I got all the feels."

Wind burst into laughter at the insanity of them all reading her manuscript in one night and at Kat using the term *feels*. "That's great. Thanks for the compliment."

"You should send this to your agent." Kat tapped the envelope.

Prickles of warning danced up the back of Wind's neck, and her breath caught. "No. My agent's right. I need to get to that audition before I lose the only part left in New York City I'll be allowed to play. I need to rebuild my reputation."

"You need to put on your big-girl panties and finish what you started here." Kat crossed her arms over her chest, and Wind knew she needed to escape before she ended up trapped by some insane attorney tactic.

"Listen, I'm glad the board liked it, but that doesn't mean it is Hollywood-worthy." Wind slid her suitcase from under the bed and flopped it onto the bed.

Jewels harrumphed but stepped aside. "You're making a mistake."

"That's okay. Don't worry. I won't let her disappoint the board by abandoning her promise to help children with special needs to have a center that will allow them to grow up and live their best lives possible. A center where, if they don't get treatment, they could end up in residential care homes for the rest of their lives."

Wind's movements stuttered with shame, but she wouldn't be guilted into it. "I've done what I promised. I fixed Rhonda's script. Not an easy task, mind you."

"No, it wasn't." Kat shrugged. "You're right. You've done your part, and no matter what I say, I won't change your mind. Because you are the stubborn great actress who is scared of no audition or part but a frightened child when it comes to life."

"Wow, Dr. Kat. Glad to know what you think of me." Wind opened a drawer and dropped some clothes into her luggage. "What do you want me to do? Live in Jewels's place forever? Well, until she finally says yes to Trevor and then I need to find a place of my own anyway."

They both shot Jewels a look.

"Stay on topic," Jewels said firmly. "We're discussing Wind running away."

"I'm not running away. I'm going to audition for a part in a play. That's what I do." Wind tossed more clothes into the bag, but Jewels took them out and put them back in the drawer.

"Stop that." Wind yanked the clothes from Jewels.

"It's okay. Let her go. I guess I'll have to let Rhonda know that she's directing the show since Wind doesn't want it."

A firebolt of anger catapulted into her chest. "What? Who? You wouldn't."

Kat smirked. "What's it going to be? Stay and face the next act in your life, or return to the only thing you know and miss out on all the possibilities ahead of you?"

Chapter Thirteen

DAMON FED Badger and collapsed into the chair he'd pulled into the kitchen. He ached in places he didn't even know his body could hurt, but he eyed the finished product. The chef's kitchen he couldn't wait to cook in and then eventually staff with a full-time chef, not to mention servers, hostesses, and bussers.

Why didn't he feel more excited about the opening? He'd come so far. He saw his dream moving closer by the day. A dream he'd held on to throughout a twenty-seven-year rocky marriage. Yet, the last week, it had only been him and Badger. Life seemed empty without Wind around. She always knew how to light up a room and keep life interesting. Without her, everything appeared cloudy with a chance of loneliness.

Badger gobbled the last few bites of his meal and lifted his head. The corner of his mouth jerked back, and a dull growl echoed through the empty restaurant.

"What's up, boy?" Damon shot up in fear he'd left the door open and some menacing reptile had found its way in.

"Anyone there?" Wes's voice carried through the dining room to the kitchen.

"Yeah. Come on in. Just make sure to close the door behind you." Damon patted Badger's head. "Good boy."

Another little growl sounded deep in his scrawny belly.

The door clicked shut and footsteps approached, so Damon tossed a treat to Badger and said, "Sit."

He did as was told and waited until Wes entered.

"Hey, man." Wes greeted him.

"You shouldn't be in here with Badger."

"No worries. Took a Benadryl." Wes eyed the iron door. "You worried Badger will get out? He's been a stray a long time. If he wants to go, maybe you should let him."

"No, scared of another gator. Besides, us two old bachelors are great company for each other. We don't have to talk or mind our manners too often." Damon eyed Wes's suit jacket. He stood in the kitchen as a well-dressed businessman, excluding baby spittle on his jacket's shoulder. Damon went to the cabinet and pulled out some baking soda.

"Understandable." Wes made a circle around the center island, gazing at each appliance and surface and boxes of pots and pans and dishes. "This place is really coming together and fast."

"I'm waiting on a few permits before I can open, not to mention hiring staff, which will be challenging. It's the one part of this I dread. I'm great with strangers but not the best at reading people."

Wes nodded with a knowing grin. "Yeah, well, you know who is?"

The wound of Wind's exit from Summer Island still felt fresh. "The woman who left for New York, you mean?" Damon pointed at Wes's jacket. "You want to take that off? I can fix the stain for you."

Wes glanced at his shoulder and let out a bolt of air. "Thought I'd escaped unscathed, but that little one has spittle superpowers." He tossed his jacket to Damon.

"Most babies do." Damon went to work putting baking soda on the stain, then using some soda water from a bottle he had since the machine wasn't ready yet.

"You seem to know what you're doing." Wes pointed at the bubbles erupting on the stain.

"Raised two of my own. One had reflux until he was two." Damon laughed at the memory. "I once attended a political rally where some woman came up and asked me if I had sat on something. I went to the bathroom and discovered when he'd hugged me goodbye that morning, he must've managed to wipe his mouth all over the back of my pants."

"Brutal." Wes leaned against the counter. "And she isn't gone."

Damon froze, unsure of what Wes meant but knew what he hoped. "Who?"

"You know who. She's been working at the Shack the last week on the play. She's there now as a matter of fact.

Says she's agreed to see the play through before she goes."

Damon's nerves twitched. Badger barked then ran to his bed, circled twice, and collapsed.

Wes clapped his hands together. "Speaking of the play... We need to have a food tasting for our top donors. It'll be four people total. Could you swing that? Say Friday at our house? Not asking you to be ready here yet or anything."

Damon eyed all the boxes. Wes must've sensed his hesitation. "Dustin and I'll swing by this Saturday to help unpack and set up anything remaining. Oh, and word has it the decking permit came through and you're good to go with that. You should get the paperwork any minute now."

"Great." Damon straightened, feeling a weight fall from him. He wiped the soda water off and handed Wes back his jacket. "Needs to dry, but should be good now."

"Thanks, man. Appreciate it." Wes took his coat but stood there for a minute longer. "And about the tasting?"

"Right. Ah, yes, of course. Send me the details. I'll need to use your kitchen and find an assistant to help out. I need to find some help for this place anyway. It'll be a good trial run for someone."

"Sounds like a great opportunity, then." Wes headed out the kitchen door. "See you Friday."

Badger whined and hopped up, looking at his leash.

"Want to go for a walk?" Damon asked.

The dog ran to the door with a bark.

"I think I could use a cup of coffee." Damon secured

the leash and headed outside, locking the door behind him. "I know you want another puppy poof thing."

Badger looked up at him and pranced forward with his head up like he'd become a real dog now that he had an owner.

They reached the Shack, and Damon reconsidered his options. He could make himself a cup of coffee at the Keurig machine in his hotel room. Maybe this was a bad idea. Wind hadn't told him she was staying, so maybe she didn't want to see him.

Badger lifted his leg and peed on the old-fashioned faux gas lamp.

"You gonna let that dog defile our good town? That mutt should be sent to the pound," Skipper shouted out of the hardware store.

Damon lifted his hand. "Sorry. Won't happen again."

Badger took off, the leash flying from Damon's hand. A car squealed to a halt inches from his new furry friend. Damon raced to catch him.

"Told you that mutt's a menace." Skipper pounded her fist into the air.

Badger didn't stop, not until he reached the Shack, where he pawed at the door. Damon hurried up the steps and pounced on the leash.

The door flew open to Wind standing over them both with a show-stopping smile. "Thought I heard Skipper shouting about a dog. You know how this town feels about strays. You better claim him or get rid of him."

"I never understood what the problem was. Homeless

doesn't make you bad." Damon took offense to them picking on his pup.

"Really? So you don't mind strays?"

"Nope." He stood, brushed off his work pants, and wrapped the leash around his wrist to make sure Badger couldn't escape this time.

"Really? So I can have animal control return your stray gator."

"Ha. A gator is nothing like a stray dog. Badger here can't bite your leg off."

"Skipper might argue since she still has that scar on her right ankle from the stray dog she tried to pet one day on the beach about two decades ago. She's as scared of dogs as you are of gators."

He hadn't heard about that. "Sorry to hear that. I'll keep Badger away from her shop."

Wind squatted down and patted Badger on the head. "Aren't you a menacing mongrel like your owner..."

"Resorting to name calling now?"

She looked up through those extra-long, extra-alluring lashes of hers. "Not calling names if it's true. Have you looked in the mirror lately?" Her nails scratched Badger's chin, and he flipped over, belly up in submission. Poor sap. She'd won him over.

"I might not be a fancy pants New Yorker, but I'm hardworking."

"You can be hardworking and not grow a beard and walk around town looking like an abandoned mutt."

Badger growled.

"Sorry. No offense."

Badger wiggled to make her resume her pet.

Damon dared a quick glance in the window to the Shack. Maybe he had let himself go, but he'd been working too hard to care. "I haven't been out much in the last week. Guess I could use a shave and haircut."

"Yeah, I know. I've been looking for you in hopes of a chance meeting."

Chance meeting? His pulse double tapped. Had she wanted to see him? Perhaps she was staying and wanted to speak with him about it. Sure, he didn't want to fall in love or commit to marriage or anything like that, but the last week without her had shown him one thing. He didn't enjoy life without her around. "You know I'm at the restaurant every day."

"Yes, but then I'd be coming to find you, and Wind Lively doesn't go out of her way. She runs into someone— ergo the chance part of the meeting."

She seemed lighter today, not as upset or broken as the last time. He wanted to ask what had changed her attitude but didn't want to get in another argument with her. "I heard you've been working on the play. How's that going?" He squatted by her side, locking gazes with her, wanting her to see he'd missed her too and that her visit would've been welcomed.

"Actually..." She eyed Badger then him. "I'd like for you to come inside. I need a favor from you." She stood and swung open the door. "And bring Badger. He's the one I really wanted to see."

Ouch. So she hadn't wanted to see him because she'd missed him but because she wanted something from him.

Inside, he found several children of various ages and Mr. Mannie. Kat stood in the far back corner near the door with Allie in her arms. She didn't seem to notice him since she was feeding her baby.

"Can everyone say hi to Mr. Reynolds?"

The kids said it in unison, filling the room with such happiness. One of the boys sat on the floor with his arms crossed, rocking and covering his ears. Another little girl, who Damon could tell had Down Syndrome, tried to cuddle the boy. Mr. Mannie stood from his chair, hunched over his cane, and with his best mimicking child-like voice, he said, "Good morning, Mr. Rude Reynolds. We were rehearsing until you interrupted."

"Down, Mr. Mannie. He's not here to stay, but Badger is. That is if Mr. Reynolds wouldn't mind sharing him with us. We need a dog for the play. I thought maybe I could use Houdini, but the diva refused to come down from his platform this morning. He apparently didn't like getting up that early. I wrote the part for a dog anyway."

Damon didn't like the idea of giving up his one companion, but with all those little eyes looking at him, he had to say something. "Um, he's not trained."

Wind shrugged. "No worries. Mr. Mannie used to work as a lion tamer for the circus. I think he can manage a dog."

Damon eyed Wind with a quirk of his brow. "Since when?"

Mr. Mannie tapped his cane twice to the hardwood floor. "Since 1954. I was the top trainer, too."

Damon knew better than to argue with the man. He was more stubborn than...than Wind. "I could stay and help."

"Don't need you making our sweet director upset. Now skedaddle."

Chapter Fourteen

THE CHILDREN GATHERED AROUND BADGER, and he ate up the attention, rolling over and wiggling with delight. Damon handed her the leash and backstepped toward the door. "Guess I'll leave him with you guys."

Wind wanted to tell him not to go...ever, but her mouth went dry and her words lodged between hope and confusion.

Marek stepped out of the pantry and waved Damon over. "Hey man."

Damon eyed the children. "They look happy. Guess I'll get a cup of coffee and hang for a bit."

"Great," Wind said. "You can watch us and tell us how you think the play is going. Sets should be done in a few days." She pressed her hand to her swishing belly. "I've not had these kinds of jitters since my first opening night."

Damon touched her arm, his rough fingers grazing her skin like a match lighting her senses. A simple touch, brief and gentle, but it ignited all the feels. "You'll do great. You're the amazing, beautiful, talented star Wind Lively, and these kids are lucky to have you."

She spied little Joey, who moved closer and closer until he sat Badger on his lap. Tina giggled and played with his paws. The other children sat around in a circle oohing and awing over the mutt. "I think it's me who's the lucky one."

Before she showed too much interest in this small-town project, she clapped her hands together and said, "Places."

The kids scrambled to their Xs she'd marked on the floor. Even Mr. Mannie found his spot as he said, "We're ready when you stop buzzing around that boy like a hungry mosquito."

Wind fought a blush rising to her cheeks. "Guess I better get back to work."

Damon nodded and moved to the counter, where he sat chatting with Marek.

Wind forced her attention back to the children. "Okay, since we have Badger here, let's practice the scenes he's in. Tina, you know what to do?"

She nodded, and her smile warmed Wind's heart. Her mother had said she was dressed this morning and waiting at the door for rehearsals an hour before she was supposed to leave. If only the patrons of her Broadway shows were so excited to see her still.

Badger ran up to the makeshift stage and sat looking forward as if he was ready for his debut. Wind shook off her weary thoughts and focused on the kids. Kids who warmed her heart and made her feel alive. She hadn't enjoyed work this much in a decade.

"Joey, you sit next to Mr. Mannie on the floor. Then Mr. Mannie stands and says—"

"I know my line," Mannie grumbled.

"Right, of course you do." Wind looked at Joey and mimed petting Badger. "Joey, then you start to slowly get closer to the dog. Mr. Mannie does his part. Then you get up and walk across the stage, where you meet Tina at that circle. The rest of the children, you sit on the floor and wave at Joey walking away."

They'd been rehearsing this one scene without a dog all morning with lots of issues, but that didn't bother Wind. Not when she knew they could do it. They just needed to believe they could.

Joey plopped down on the floor without a word and eyed Badger.

Mannie cleared his throat and waited for the rest of the kids to settle. The cranky old man looked disgruntled at having to work with such distractions, but Wind knew better. He loved every minute of being around these special children.

"Begin when ready, Mannie." She stepped back away from center stage, and Joey blinked at her. She knew he was nervous. "Don't worry. You can do this." She did two thumbs-up, and he smiled and mimicked her gesture.

Mannie's stern expression remained. "Kid, whatcha want? Why don't you talk none?"

Joey curled into himself and scooted from Mannie.

Wind wasn't sure if it was acting or a response to Mannie. Apparently Mannie noticed too, so his face softened and he sat down in the chair. "This here's my friend. Like me, he doesn't like most people."

Joey didn't budge, and Mannie patted Badger's head. The dog scooted toward Joey on his belly, paws outstretched in front of him. Wow, that dog could act.

"He doesn't like people because people don't understand him. He doesn't look like the other dogs or behave like other dogs. He's kind of scruffy and a reject."

Joey blinked up at him, his face coming alive with a small smile. He looked to Badger then reached out to touch his paw with one finger. Badger lowered his muzzle to the ground and scooted even closer. Joey scooted closer to the dog. They inched toward each other until Badger put his muzzle on Joey's lap.

Mannie tapped his cane, softer than normal after she'd explained Joey didn't like sudden movements or loud sounds. "Never seen him take to nobody like that before. You must be special."

Joey lifted his chin but didn't say anything. He never spoke in the play or anywhere else in public. Something the therapists hoped to work on with him. Wind would be cheering him on throughout his therapy, even if it would be from afar. Her chest ached at not seeing these kids daily anymore. She felt like part of their lives now.

She dared a quick glance at Damon, who appeared to be enthralled with their little production.

Mannie leaned forward and lowered his glasses,

staring down at Joey. "Well, I'll be darned. Guess you've got to be my friend now too, 'cause I'm too old to take Badger for walks and he needs the exercise. You think you can take him up the street and back for me?"

Joey gave an exaggerated nod then shuffled to his feet and took the leash from Mannie.

"Thank you. You're a good helper."

Joey lifted his chin and turned to find the circle, his eyes trained on his mark, never looking out from the stage, but that didn't matter. She'd never make him look out at the audience if he didn't want to, because this wasn't about being perfect. This play was about educating others.

She held her breath as he shuffled to his mark with Badger by his side.

Tina came out and lowered, but the dog growled at her. Wind jolted forward, not sure about Tina's safety. But she was a star up there. "Guess he doesn't trust me. If we were friends, maybe he'd trust me. Want to be my friend?"

Joey nodded and looked over his shoulder at Mannie, then to Badger, and then to Tina. Wind held her breath, willing Joey to say the word yes aloud, but he only nodded and went off stage with her.

"Perfect," Mannie shouted. "Joey and Tina were brilliant."

Wind clapped, more to get Joey used to the noise, and she eyed Damon and Marek, who joined her. Damon whistled loud. Joey cringed but then looked to Damon and bowed. Her heart soared to a new height. The little boy who didn't interact with others just communicated with a stranger. Maybe not with words, but he connected.

She went to the stage and knelt in front of Joey and Tina. "You both were brilliant. Perfect. You do that the day of the show, and you'll wow this entire town."

Joey passed the leash to her, his eyes fading from the world again, and he retreated to his corner, where he rocked back and forth. She knew he needed a break from the attention, so she told everyone to take five and went to where Kat joined Marek and Damon at the counter.

"I have a question. I'm not a therapist, but I read up on children with sensory issues, and some respond well to weighted vests to keep them calm—or earmuffs, or other things. Joey is going to be on sensory overload on the night of the play. All those eyes looking at him might be too much. Could you ask one of the therapists if there are any tools we can use? I don't want to stress him out more than necessary."

Damon leaned back in his chair and tapped his cup. "Look at you."

"What?" Wind scanned her clothes from the top button of her polka dot shirt to her black sandals with silver sequins. Nothing was out of place.

"You're a natural with those kids. I mean, how did you get to this point with them? That was amazing. You have a gift."

Kat bounced Allie on her lap. "I knew she was the right woman. She raised all her brothers and sisters, and some were challenging at times, yet she never complained about it. Well, except the responsibility of being a mother at a young age. Yet any time one of her siblings had something like this or a sporting event, she'd be there cheering them on. She never missed a beat."

Damon looked at her as if for the first time. His gaze fixed on her like a gun to a target. She squirmed under his attention.

"Thanks. But it isn't me. It's those kids. They are so special, but not in the way the world thinks. They are such gifts straight from heaven. I love each of them."

Mannie tapped his cane. "It's almost nap time for me. We gonna get this show on the move or what?"

Wind forced herself to return her attention to the world beyond Damon. "Right. Coming." She faced Damon, not wanting to end their conversation or that look she'd never seen him give her before. A look of...admiration, joy...pride? Was he proud of her? She wanted to know what that look was, and she'd find out, but now wasn't the time. "I know you have a lot to do. How about I bring Badger to the restaurant after we're done here?"

"Perfect." His gaze scanned the length of her, and the strange look snapped back to the familiar passion but with a dash of softness this time.

"Great. See you then." Wind returned to the others and forced herself to keep her mind on the play and not her wayward thoughts of a man who ran hotter than the sun and colder than dry ice all in a breath of time.

Chapter Fifteen

DAMON ABANDONED his work on the menu to pace and pace and pace around the tables, carefully placed in a strategic way. A way that allowed for the most seats without crowding. The same way he'd constructed his life.

He remembered how Wind had moved, guiding the kids on stage like a conductor to a world-class orchestra. She came alive the way he remembered her from years ago. It's what originally attracted him to her and also drove him away.

The air conditioning cut on, sending a blast of cooling air over him. He eyed the menu and decided he'd practice a few since he'd picked up the ingredients. A trial run before tomorrow night. Since he was going to cook, why not set the table to practice that too. He placed the candles in the center of the table, then returned to his food prep. Tuna tartare, cool and refreshing and easy to prepare as an appetizer, followed by pepper-crusted pork tenderloin medallions, and then finished with chocolate lava cakes. They were always a fan favorite.

A distant bark drew him to the front door. He opened it to see Wind walking Badger toward him. Her zillion-dollar smile and distracting sway of her hips were a beautiful contrast to the softness she'd shown with the children. Wind Lively, great with kids. He'd always thought she hated children after having to care for her siblings so long. What else had he gotten wrong about her?

"Hey, you. One dog returned unharmed. Well, except for Joey squeezing him goodbye. That boy is mesmerized by the fur on your pup here. You've done a great job cleaning him up. He almost looks presentable."

Badger barked at her.

"Sorry! Didn't mean to offend. I meant it as a compliment." She winked at Badger.

Damon stepped to the side and waved to the restaurant. "Please come inside."

She eyed the door then him, and he knew he had to convince her to enter before she ran off.

"I could use your help with the menu I'm preparing for Saturday." Damon's heart beat harder than the afternoon thunder that rolled into the island on hot evenings.

"Sure. I do love food." She shrugged.

He wiped the sweat that pooled at his brow and shut the door behind her. "You were great with those kids."

"You sound so surprised." Wind unhooked Badger's leash, and he scampered to the kitchen, probably looking for his treats.

"I'm never surprised that you're good at something. I guess I always thought you...I don't know..." He toed the ground, scared to say what he really thought since he didn't want to spark an argument.

"That I hated children." Wind crossed the room, eyeing the walls, ceiling, floor, tables, and him. "I get why you'd think that. I mean, I couldn't wait to escape from my parental duties, but I was a teenager asked to care for my siblings. I loved them, but I wanted my own life. Besides, I was never really the right kind of kid in that family. I was too boisterous, combative, curious..."

"Exceptional." Damon clenched his jaw, but it was too late. He'd already said it, and based on her wide-eyed expression, she'd heard the want in his tone.

Wind tilted her head, that gorgeous ginger hair brushing across her cheek. "Thank you," she breathed.

He wanted to touch her, pull her close, show her how much he'd missed her this last week.

She cleared her throat. "I'm so glad we can be friends now."

A dagger of rejection pierced him faster than gator teeth. "Friends. Right." He clenched his fist and bopped her on the shoulder. "Well, friend. Care to help with the tasting?"

She eyed the table set for two and smiled. "I'd be delighted."

Cool air shot from the overhead vent, causing the petals of the single flower in the crystal vase to flutter.

"I thought I'd test the environment too. You see, I want

to have a romantic dining room, with fun and casual deck seating outside. Inside date night, outside friends." He stumbled over his words and bumbled his thoughts. "But we're eating inside because...because—"

"There isn't a deck." Wind sauntered by him. "A friend who's a gentleman should still pull out a chair for a lady."

"Right. Of course." He grabbed the back of the chair and yanked it across the floor with a loud squeal. "Guess I need to put some felt pads under the feet. See, test runs are a good idea."

"Right. I agree."

"I'll be right back. First course is tuna tartare."

"I'm allergic."

He sucked in a quick breath. "What?"

"Just kidding, friend." Wind removed the cloth napkin and placed it on her lap. "Do you need help in the kitchen?"

"No. Thank you, though. I only made two appetizers and a few pork medallions and cake. Wanted to test things out for the food tasting with the major donors to the center on Friday."

"I'm glad I could be of service." Her voice carried like a Julie Andrews tune to the kitchen. His daughter had always loved *The Sound of Music*.

He plated the tuna and the pork then returned to the dining room to find the candles lit and the lights down low. Slow, sensual music played from Wind's phone.

"Test run for the romantic dining room, right?"

His mouth went Cabernet dry. "Right." He set the plates down on the table before he dropped them. Wind had removed her sweater, revealing more skin than he'd seen in a while. The woman had stayed fit. Of course she had, with all that dancing she'd been doing all these years.

"Are you going to gawk all night or sit down and eat with me?" Wind picked up her fork and pierced a piece of tuna and avocado then ate it with a moan. "Wow, delicious."

Her compliment warmed his insides. "Thank you."

She scooped up another bite, and with her palm under it as if in fear of spilling, she held it out for him. "Here, you need to taste your own creation."

He took the offered bite and savored the tangy yet salty flavor.

She leaned in with her napkin and dabbed at the corner of his mouth. "Had a little there."

He didn't know how long he would be able to sit here, alone, with the amazing Wind Lively, pretending to only think of her as a friend, but that's what he'd said. That's what he wanted. "Wind. I have a confession to make."

Badger trotted over and sat on his hind legs, looking up expectantly.

"No, back into bed. You've been fed."

The dog bowed his head and ran back to the corner to sulk.

"Confession?" She rested her elbow on the table and cupped her chin in her hand.

"Yes. I was sad when I thought you'd left for New York. I missed you."

"You did?" Wind leaned back and picked up her fork. "It's nice to know that you care about your friends."

He let out a gust of air, causing the candles to flicker. "Stop."

"Stop what?"

"Playing games." He scooted his chair around the table and turned her to face him.

"I'm not the one playing games. You are. The way you look at me contradicts what you tell me. I'm a grown woman, not some teenager who can't pick up on facial expressions and body language. You want me, but you tell yourself you don't."

"Oh, I can't deny that I'm attracted to you. That was never our problem. But we didn't work."

"Why didn't we work? It was so long ago I can't remember. All I know is that you told me we'd never be happy together after dating for a couple of months. Then we spent the next several months stealing glances and trying to avoid each other until I left for New York. Then I returned and you kissed me, and then you told me that you didn't want anything with me. Now does that sound like I'm the one playing games, or you?"

He scrubbed his face as if to clean the mistakes from his skin then looked at her. "You're right. I need to be honest with you and myself. I ended things back then because I knew I'd never make you happy. You were destined for greatness, to be a star, and I never wanted that life. I didn't want to be with a woman I'd hold back. My mother was held back by my father her entire life. I know she regretted not getting a job and always having to rely on my father for her so-called allowance. I never wanted to be that man."

She closed her eyes. "After all this time. I thought I'd left you because I was scared of being a stay-at-home mom. I couldn't be my mother, having so many kids I couldn't raise them all on my own and had to rely on my eldest daughter to help."

"I guess we both had our reasons."

"We did then, but what about now? You said you were worried about losing yourself because you'd already given your life to helping your ex-wife and now you only want this restaurant."

"Yes, that's true. I think I tried so hard not to be my father that I became a person I don't recognize. I sacrificed so much to make my wife happy until I wasn't happy and the marriage fell apart. I'm just as much to blame as Angela was. I should've said no a long time ago. When I finally did, she didn't understand the word. I came here because every time I saw her, she'd ask me to pose in a picture with her or help her write her next speech."

"No can be one of the most difficult words to use." Wind covered his hand, sending a thousand fireflies buzzing in his gut. "Look, I got suckered into writing a script and directing a kids' play because I couldn't say no to Kat."

He scooted to the edge of his chair and cupped her

cheek. "But you're brilliant at it. You're brilliant at everything."

"Listen, I don't know what I'm going to do after the show, but I know I'd never expect you to give up your dream for me."

"I know you wouldn't. I trust you. It was me I didn't trust. I gave and gave and gave, and the only way I didn't feel like my father but could escape pleasing someone was to keep my distance. I became good at keeping my distance."

"And now? Now do you want to keep your distance?"

"No."

His pulse drummed. Heart hammered. He grazed her soft skin with his fingertips, giving her one last chance to pull away, but she didn't. And that was all the invitation he needed. Swept up in all that was the woman of his past, present, and possible future, he let his grip on reality slip, and he grazed her ear with his lips. "Last chance to run."

She shivered but didn't move away. "Hon, I've never been the type to run."

He slid his mouth down her jawline to the edge of her lips, where he paused and nibbled, remembering their last kiss and every kiss they'd ever shared because each was unique and epic.

Badger's whine faded. Candles flickered. The world slowed and stopped around them. Stopped long enough for him to taste the promise of a better tomorrow. He tilted her chin up and captured her in a deep, passionate, all-consuming kiss.

Chapter Sixteen

THE ELECTRIC CONNECTION Wind shared with Damon charged her body to a full storm. She felt like her life truly began in that moment. The moment that Damon finally surrendered to her.

Breathless, intoxicated by his strong frame and pulse-skipping touch, she threw her arms around him and pulled him tight. Her skin flushed, and she thought she'd never let go but couldn't hold on another moment without losing herself forever.

They broke apart. Foreheads resting on each other, eyes closed, panting, clutching hands. Wind's mind churned but with nothing. A swirling, brewing, whirlwind of nothingness because she never wanted to think another thought beyond that kiss.

"Wow. That was *Casablanca* good," she mumbled through the fog but didn't dare open her eyes in fear of breaking the spell.

"No, that was Wind Lively and Damon Reynolds good. Ingrid Bergman has nothing on you."

His hand slipped from her face, but she caught it and held it to her heart. "Wait, don't move. Not yet."

"Wind, I'm not going anywhere. I'm not running away. I've got this restaurant. And I've got you for as long as you stay in Summer Island."

His voice cracked, shattering her to pieces. Did he want her to stay? Could she stay?

"I never want to compete with your dreams. I'd never stand in your way."

"My dreams are changing. I never wanted to be a stay-at-home mom, so we never would've worked out before, but what about now? Now, I want more out of life beyond the stage, beyond make believe. I want something real."

"I'm real."

"That you are." She giggled and dared to open her eyes, sitting back to see him only inches away. She didn't want to end their moment before it ran half the race, but she couldn't help but ask. If he was going to push her away again, she needed to know now. "What's next?"

"Next?" He took his free hand and picked up a fork, pierced a piece of pork, and held it up to her mouth. "We figure out a menu for the fundraiser, and we work together to make sure the show goes off without any issues. We'll work together as a team."

"I'd like that." Wind took a bite. The peppery, hearty goodness coated her tongue, but the joyous taste held nothing to Damon's kisses. "Mmmm. I think your restaurant is going to be a hit."

"I hope so. I sank a lot into this place. I'd hate to blow it now." He took a bite of his own, and they sat at the bistro table, listening to Badger snore in the corner, the wind blowing outside, and soft music playing.

For hours they talked, held hands, and kissed until Wind knew she had to get back before Jewels sent Houdini after her.

Damon walked her home, and they stood on the front porch, Houdini scratching at the window playing chaperone. "He's an interesting little critter, isn't he?"

"You have no idea. That little man knows everything about everyone and is always meddling. He's more of a diva than I am."

He closed in on her, his look powerful, his hands gripping hers. "You're not a diva, and don't let anyone put you down ever again. Especially not me. You're a kind woman with a heart of gold. I saw you with those kids, and I couldn't deny it any longer. You're an amazing, beautiful, and talented woman."

"I thought you found me self-absorbed and flighty."

He bowed his head into a position like a bad dog. "No, I never believed it. I only said that to keep my distance because you're so much, Wind."

"I know. I'm too much at times."

He pulled her into his arms and hugged her tight against him, resting his chin on her head. "No. You're perfect. That was the problem. I couldn't give my heart to you because I didn't know if I could ever get it back if you walked away. But now I realized even if I can only have you for a moment, that's better than never."

"What if I stay?" She said the words she'd been thinking. With his confession, how could she not be equally as brave?

He kissed the top of her head, her cheek, her lips. "Don't say that. I can't even think it. I'll come to see you in New York. We'll figure out a way to spend time together when we can. I just can't believe you'll stay here. You don't belong in small-town Florida. You belong in big city lights. And I never wanted to hold you back from that."

She knew she couldn't return to New York. Not to some bit part off Broadway. Maybe it was time to retire and try to work on her scripts again. Who cared what her agent said. She'd fired former agents for less than dismissing her dreams. "I'll see you in the morning."

"You better."

"And every morning after that. I promise, I'm not going anywhere."

He opened his mouth, but she stole another kiss to silence him. When she managed to break away again, she whispered in his ear, "I promise. I'm staying." Before he could argue, she rushed inside and shut the door.

"It's about time," Jewels said.

Wind turned to find Jewels, Trace, and Kat all sitting in the small living room, smiling up at her. "Better now than never. Because now is the perfect time."

Chapter Seventeen

THREE GLORIOUS DAYS Damon spent enjoying kisses from Wind away from the town's prying eyes. Of course, he never thought they'd keep their relationship a secret for long, but they felt like teenagers again sneaking around.

Trevor helped carry supplies from his car into Kat and Wes's massive mansion. Damon had heard it was nice, but this was ridiculous. Ridiculously gorgeous.

Damon scanned the horizon and inhaled the ocean air. Even from a few blocks away, it was clean and refreshing. "The sky looks even bluer today if that's possible."

Trevor laughed so loudly it echoed into the front door of the house.

"What?"

"You're in love, buddy." He grabbed another box, stacked it on top of the first, and then lifted them both.

"Please, we just started dating again, and who knows what will happen." Damon told himself that every day, but he wouldn't let the fear stand in his way of now. How many more moments would he get in this world where a woman made him feel this way? There had to be an expiration date on feeling in love and alive, the way his joints ached less and his body stood taller. He hadn't reached his shelf life yet, though.

Wind stood in the kitchen wearing an apron blinged out with rhinestones with ruffled sleeves. He only knew those terms from raising a daughter. He slid the box onto the counter and took both her hands. "You look stunning as always." He planted a kiss on her lips for all to see. Okay, their close friends anyway.

"Hey, enough of that. You two are here to work, not play kissy-face." Kat tapped her tablet with the stylus and eyed them with a stern gaze and a mischievous smile.

"Right, work." Damon unpacked his supplies and forced himself to concentrate on his culinary duties instead of his heart's desire. Wait. The culinary life was his heart's desire. A warning pricked in the back of his mind that he was doing it again, putting a woman before his dreams. He needed to remain focused and work on his personal goals while enjoying Wind's company. Balance. That's what he needed, and he'd figure it out. Because Wind would never get in the way of achieving his dreams. He trusted her.

"Stop overthinking." Wind folded the cloth napkins into little birds and set them aside. "You'd think you were the girl in this relationship."

"I can assure you, I'm a full-blooded man."

"Keep it G, buddy. This is a children's fundraising

event." She flicked a napkin at him, snapping at his arm with a short sting.

"Hey, I'll pay you back for that later. For now, work."

"Wow, I've worked for directors less bossy than you." Wind folded another napkin.

"Need any help in there?" Kat called out from the living room.

"No. All good."

"Remember, our guests are important people we need to impress so we can acquire more funds for the center."

"Got it." He saluted and then whispered to Wind, "I've worked for politicians less aggressive than her."

"I heard that."

Damon started the burners, mixed sauces, and diced vegetables while Wind worked alongside him as his sous-chef. He couldn't find an assistant in time so he had Wind step in to help. Not that he'd ever really tried. He savored each moment. They worked together well in the kitchen. If she wasn't a gifted actress, he'd try to hire her to work in his restaurant. Everyone would love her, and he could use the help. Yet, that would never happen. At best, he hoped to see her between shows and when she came home for holidays. It would have to be enough.

"Who's watching Badger tonight?" Wind asked.

"Tabitha. Marek said she's taken with him and is now asking for a dog of her own. He told her to see what she thought about taking care of a dog before they got one."

"Smart man."

"Yes, he is." Damon tossed the onions in to sauté.

Steam rose to the fan and disappeared. The chef's kitchen. "This space is top of the line. Do they cook a lot?"

"Not really." Wind shrugged. "Baby and business take up most of their time."

"I remember those days." He chuckled.

She studied the carrots a little too intently.

"What is it? Do you regret not having children?"

"No. Not at all." Wind shrugged. "I was thinking that Kat has it all and is happy here. She gave up her insanely high-paying and prestigious position to start a center for special needs children, and I've never seen her happier. It's how I used to feel when I stepped on a stage."

The onions turned translucent, so he added more to the pan, and soon the room filled with the hearty, mouth-watering aroma. "But you don't feel that anymore?"

"No. Well, not on stage." She nibbled on a julienned carrot. "I did while working with the kids, though. That sense of not knowing what could happen on stage in my early years always kept me focused and ready to adjust and change and move to keep the audience engaged, but in recent years nothing new ever happens. I think that scathing review I received was my own fault. I've been blaming the newspaper for ruining my career, but honestly, I have no one to blame but myself. I didn't feel the passion, and I went through the motions. I lied to the audience, and they saw through me."

"Can you return now and wow your fans again?" He shoulder bumped her. "You wow me every day."

She passed him the sauce but didn't let go of the bowl. "Could I, yes...maybe. But do I want to?"

"Do you?" He held his breath. Maybe she could find her happiness here, working for the center or directing small-town plays.

"I don't know." She relinquished the bowl. "I won't lie to you or myself. I've always needed the big adventure, the uncertainty, the feeling of being alive and unsure of what was next in my life. Long-term, will I be happy here in a small beachside town?"

The doorbell rang, warning Damon he needed to concentrate and finish up his appetizers. He went into double-time mode, and she worked seamlessly with him by her side. When he plated the last hors d'oeuvres, she stalled his hand with her light touch.

"And in this kitchen. This is new and exciting to me."

He kissed her cheek. "You're welcome in my kitchen anytime."

"I warned you two. Work, no fraternizing. You two are volatile, and I don't need drama tonight." Kat snagged a plate, handed it to Bri, and ushered her out to serve their guests.

The entire Friendster and Manster groups turned out to show their support. "And your friends. I can't imagine you having any better in New York than these guys and gals."

"No one compares to the family I have here." Wind sighed. "I think I might let my agent go and submit to another one I spoke to that thought playwriting would be a natural step in the evolution of my career. The good news is that I can stick around here longer to give myself a chance to see if this place will work for me long-term."

"Sounds great."

"I told you I wouldn't go anywhere. You should've believed me." She winked.

Kat returned to the kitchen, her face whiter than the bird-shaped napkins.

Wind was at her side in a heartbeat. "What is it? What's going on?"

"The center. We were just informed that our funding from the state was pulled. Some new politician has changed something, and now the grant money is gone. Even with all the donations, we won't be able to run it without the grant money. Two donors just told me they would be pulling their support since that funding isn't coming through."

Damon froze. "Something smells fishy, and it isn't my tuna tartare."

"What do you mean?"

Approaching were two men dressed in important-looking suits.

"I'll tell you later. Not now."

One of the men with shiny silver hair offered his hand. "This food is perfect. I, for one, will be bringing clients to your restaurant in the future for business meetings. Also, my wife will be hiring you for a private event at our estate."

"I look forward to hearing from you both." Damon shook his hand, feeling a little dirty, the way he'd felt during his days as the senator's husband. All the back-alley deals and empty promises always made him feel less of a man.

He cleaned up the counter, listening to all the uppity-ups speak about being supportive yet with several conditions. As the night meandered on, his chest ached at the sight of Wind's disappointment and the thought of the children.

She wiped down the counter with tears in her eyes. He cuddled her into his side and kissed the top of her head. "Don't worry. We'll figure something out."

"I'm not upset for me but for the children. No way I want to tell them that all their hard work was for nothing."

"We'll put on that play even if it isn't part of the fundraiser."

Wind smiled up at him. "You claim to only care about your own goals, but that heart of yours is too big and too special to ignore anyone around you. Don't worry about the play. I'll figure it out. You keep focus on the restaurant's opening."

Wind had surprised him again. He'd been so wrong about her.

The door closed on the last guest, and all the Friendsters, Mansters, and even Kat's mom, a new honorary member like himself, sat in the living room making plans.

Wind leaned into him sitting on the sofa, the warmth of her body soothing his anxiety. "Don't worry. Your restaurant will be fine. I'll make sure Skipper doesn't block any zoning or permits or inspections for your opening."

"I'm not worried about my restaurant."

Trace paced the floor until Dustin pulled her to sit in his lap. She swished her lips then looked around the room. "Why would the grant money be reappropriated? And what was it reappropriated for? Maybe we can take it to social media and show the big political mess that took away our children's future. Brand them as the traitors they are."

"Down, Ms. Activist. We have local politicians who made this center happen. We don't want to alienate everyone," Kat said.

Damon cleared his throat, drawing everyone's attention. He didn't want to dip his toe into the pool of the elite, because he found it chilly, but he needed to help. "Listen, I've had a lot of experience in politics, and I guarantee this budget issue is buried beneath something and exchanged for a favor."

"Meaning?" Kat asked, a flicker of hope sparking in her eyes.

"Meaning that when someone asks for something in politics, especially at that level, there is some back-alley bargaining going on. This grant money must've been offered to one person so that they could reciprocate with something else. We need to figure out who and how someone did this. Especially for a grant that had already been given to other institutions."

"Why?" Wes ran a hand through his hair, his brows furrowed. "Budgetary cuts. That's what they told us. Legally there is nothing we can do to fight this." He looked to his wife, who nodded in confirmation.

"That's the standard answer. We need the truth." One glance at Wind, and he knew he had to do everything in his power to make this right. Even if it meant selling his own soul to his ex. "And I know where to go to get the answer."

Wind covered her mouth then snagged his elbow, pulling him closer to her. "No, you don't have to do that."

He rubbed his temple. "If anyone else has any other options, let me know. I'd love to step aside."

Everyone looked at one another.

He slapped his knees and stood. "Then I guess I better go make that call." A call that opened the door to his own back-room dealings. Dealings that he knew would inevitably take him away from Summer Island. Away from his restaurant. Away from his new friends. Away from Wind.

Chapter Eighteen

WIND TOSSED and turned and tormented herself all night. She needed to figure something out to save the center. Certainly, after all those years of admirers in New York, she could figure out someone she could call.

She got up to watch the sunrise but missed it while she scrolled through her contacts on her phone, hoping to find some sort of thread she could pull to unravel this nightmare. This place, it was too important. What would Joey do since his mother didn't have the insurance to help pay for the therapy? She'd spent most of her life with inferior help and struggling to put food on the table. The play had unlocked him enough to socialize. His own mother couldn't believe how much he'd done in such a short time compared to all that time in the special needs classroom.

And what about Sarah Jane, who wanted to be an actress but thought she'd never be able to due to her speech issues? And Paul who struggled to walk due to his cerebral palsy and was socially isolated from the other children at school because he was different? No. She wouldn't let this center fail.

"Hey, I thought I'd find you here." Damon trudged through the sand.

"Where's Badger?"

"That lazy old man wouldn't get out of bed this morning. I'll head back to walk him in a few." He sat by her side and handed her a plastic cup with the eye-opening smell of fresh-brewed coffee.

"Thanks. I haven't had a morning cup because I didn't want to wake Jewels."

"She didn't go home last night."

Wind raised a brow at him. "Our sweet Jewels stayed out all night with Trevor? The scandal."

"I'm pretty sure the SIBL blew up around three a.m." He wrapped his arm around her shoulders and kissed her cheek. "If you were a good friend, you'd give them something else to talk about."

"Slow down there, boy. I'm not that kind of girl."

Damon chuckled. "Now, we both know that's not true. Remember when we woke up around this spot at midnight?"

"You mean when my father trudged across this sand with his old army rifle, a flashlight, and a cross."

"I thought he was going to exorcise the demon right out of me, and I hadn't done anything wrong. Trust me. I wanted to, but we were innocent that night." He winked.

She swatted his chest. "Listen, seriously, I'm going to

make some calls today. I have a lot of old admirers I can call on, not to mention some friends up in New York who have connections."

He sighed and ran a hand through his hair. "Don't worry about it. I know how to get the information we need."

"No. I won't let you get sucked back into your ex-wife's world."

Damon tugged her tighter against him as if he feared losing her. "Don't worry. I'm not married to her anymore, so I don't feel like I have to sacrifice myself for her. Funny how it's taken all these years for me to see the truth."

"That you were a loyal and giving husband?" Wind threaded her fingers between his. "You're a good man. There is no reason to think you did anything wrong. Your wife chose her career over you."

"But I could've stood up and said no from day one. It takes two to ruin a marriage, trust me. Part of me thinks we were a placeholder for each other, a tool in our lives. She gave me two beautiful children, and I gave her a political career."

"And you wouldn't have had children with me." She studied his hand and wished things would be easier for once. "I can't say I'm sorry, though. The decision to not have children was the right one for me. I apologized for that choice for years to my family, but then I stopped because I knew I couldn't bring a baby into this world to make someone else happy."

"It's one of the things I love about you. You can stand up for yourself."

"Oh, you stand up for yourself plenty. You just chose to be the man your father wasn't. I think we tend to over-compensate for what we perceive our parents' failings are. You committed and put everything you had into a marriage to prove you weren't your father, and I ran away to avoid any permanent ties to prove I wasn't a submissive woman with no choices but to make babies."

He kissed her knuckles one at a time, and her entire arm warmed. "You're so wise."

"Shhh. Don't tell anyone. I like playing the ditzy, self-absorbed type. Then people don't expect too much from me." She shifted onto her knees, but the right one wouldn't turn that way anymore, so she stretched them out in front of her and cupped both his cheeks. "So tell me more."

"About what?"

"About what else you love about me. Remember, it's all about me all the time."

"You're going to make me regret everything I've ever said to you, aren't you?"

"I tell you what. For every time you tried to push me away since you arrived, you owe me a kiss."

"I owe you a lot of kisses, then."

"That's the idea."

He wrapped his arms around her and pulled her onto his lap. His kisses and strength and passion made her body heat beyond the spotlight by the end of a show. Her pulse sped, heartbeat pounded, desire swelled until she thought she'd go mad with desire. She pressed a hand to his chest and took in several breaths to regain her thoughts.

"There are so many things I love about you, Wind Lively, but I think there is only one that matters." He pressed his hand to her chest. "Your heart."

"You mean the one pounding like an Irish dancer on six gallons of caffeine?" She covered his hand and rested her head against his. "What are we doing?"

Damon brushed her hair away from her face and smiled the biggest, brightest smile she'd ever seen. "I don't know, but I like it. I almost hate the fact I have to go."

"Go? Why so early?"

He kissed her cheek with a quick brush of his lips and gently settled her next to him before he stood and brushed sand from his pants. "I've got to take a call."

"At this hour?"

"It's the only free time she has today. She'll be in meetings and luncheons and all sorts of events the rest of the week."

Wind jumped up. "Wait. No. If you're going to speak to your wife to get help, don't. I told you, I'm going to figure something out."

"Don't worry. I'm only going to ask her to dig into this and find out who interfered with the funding. She can get us a real answer, not a generic one. We need information if we want to fight this."

"But Kat is already looking into new grants today. I'm going to call in some favors. Trace even has some connections she's going to reach out to. Between all of us, we'll figure it out. You don't have to throw yourself on your sword again."

He ran his fingers from her elbow to her wrist, leaving a trail of electricity behind. "You said it. We'll all be making calls. Including me."

Wind wanted to stop him from having to reconnect with the world he'd worked so hard to break free of. "You told me that she'd do anything to bring you back in as her supporter. Won't this open the door for that? What about your restaurant?"

"All I want is information. That'll cost me one public appearance. I'm no longer the dutiful husband trying to overcompensate for daddy issues. This will be a business transaction. Nothing more."

She clung to him. Something deep inside told her not to let him go this time. "Then let me be with you when you talk to her."

He chuckled and squeezed her fingers. "Don't worry. I have no romantic feelings for Angela anymore. I only have eyes for you."

"You think I'm jealous?" *Oh dear Lord, am I?* "Wind Lively doesn't get jealous. I'm only worried for you."

He skirted his lips along her cheek to her ear. "Good, because I could never find another woman like you."

His warm breath caressed her ear and her heart. "As long as you know it." She swatted at him, forcing the Jolly Green Giant of jealousy from her mind. "Call me later?"

"Of course." He walked away and took her heart with him.

Chapter Nineteen

THE MORNING AIR filtered through the large window at the ocean-facing wall. Damon stood taking in deep, calming breaths. Wind was right. Angela would try to suck him back into her world. The woman could teach a doctorate program on manipulation. She'd do anything to get him to reconcile for the camera. A married woman with a successful family had a far better shot at the presidential ticket than a divorcee. There would be a price for this favor, but he couldn't let Wind down. He'd never agree to a reunion farse.

Badger lifted his head and let out a big yawn then stood as if at attention.

"Let's get this over with, buddy."

With one last inhale, he called his ex-wife and prepared for battle. He had a plan, a list of what he'd be willing to do for the information, and a hard line not to cross. It didn't matter if he kept the peace because he didn't have to preserve a peaceful environment for his children any longer.

"You're up strangely early. Good morning," Angela said in an unusually cheerful tone.

Badger growled low and deep. Apparently, he felt about the same as Damon did about this conversation.

"Right. Good morning." He refused to let down his guard. She had to be toying with him. Direct and straight down to business. That was the plan and one she'd respect. No time for feelings to get in the way. "Listen, I have a deal for you. Serena said you wanted me to do one photo shoot to show my support for your presidential run. In return, I'd like you to do a favor for me."

"Yes, I'll help with the kids' place your friends are working on."

He froze. "Wait. How did you know about that?"

"Serena. I saw her yesterday. What exactly do you need?"

He inhaled a quick breath and shot into his proposal mode. "I need you to find out who pulled the grant money for the special needs center. I'll email you all the details."

She gulped something, probably her early morning jug of coffee. "This center is something important to you? Did you say it was for special needs? Is this for children?"

"Yes, and—"

"I'm happy to check into it for you. And, Damon, no payment necessary. I know you think all I care about is my job, but I still care about you. It wasn't just my drive that ended our marriage. I think I sought fulfillment through my career because I knew you always had a heart for someone else."

Here they went again. The passing-the-buck game. "I never—"

"No, you were the perfect husband. I'm not saying otherwise. I'm saying it was my insecurities that got in our way. I know you might not realize this, but I do have feelings."

Some frantic sounds and grumbling echoed in the background. Badger barked.

"Shh, boy."

"Well, duty calls. Send me the details, and I'll get right on it for you. No payment necessary. If, in the future, you don't mind writing an article or standing up for a picture, great, but not because you owe me. Okay?"

He froze, eyeing the morning sun peering through the clouds as if he'd finally found the light of day. "Okay. And, uh, thanks, Angie," he said, his tone sincere.

Click.

Badger trotted over and sat at his feet.

"Well, that was unexpected."

He lifted his nose, as if proud of protecting Damon from his ex. Apparently, dogs did sense when their masters were stressed. With the phone call out of the way, he went to work at his laptop, making sure all the permits were taken care of, and then he dug into the outrageous world of grants. Pages upon pages upon pages of information but little on how to get them.

Badger hopped up and darted for the door, whining.

"You need to go out?" Damon rose to find the door opening and a tentative Wind sticking her head inside.

"Sorry to intrude. I thought I'd bring you some lunch."

"Lunch?" He glanced at his watch. "Wow, I had no idea it was that late."

She joined him at the table with his notes and laptop. "What's all this?"

"My attempt at helping." He gestured to the chair for her to sit down. "Wes and Kat are the smartest people I know, but relying on one big grant doesn't seem like the wisest move."

"They didn't. Trust me, they tried to apply for so many, but they're a new venture, so they're trying to educate the powers that be on what they're offering. Everyone knows our insurance is awful in this country and it's our children that are suffering, but they don't know what to do. Wes and Kat are revolutionizing health care for children, and not everyone is on board." She covered his hand, and his body warmed like he stood on the beach feeling the first rays of the morning sun on his skin.

"I know I'm overstepping here. I just can't stand the idea that something this important could fall apart before it starts."

Wind patted his hand then opened the brown bag and took out a few sandwiches probably from the Shack. "Didn't go well with Angela?"

He tilted his head and studied her expression. "That's why you brought lunch. You wanted to know how I felt after I spoke to her."

"And here I was thinking I'm a good actress." Wind winked.

He slid his arm around her back and nuzzled her neck. "Hon, there is no other woman now that I finally get to be with you."

"Flattery will get you a sandwich and the truth." She stiffened in his arms.

He sat back, his body rigid with concern. "What truth?"

She set down an apple and faced him, her shoulders nearly to her ears and her gaze darting around before it settled on him. "The truth that I'm scared for caring about a man who's haunted every date I've ever been on with the memory of perfection. That my heart beats fast and my pulse races every time I even think about you. That I enjoyed cooking with you more than I enjoy being on stage. The rush I felt in the kitchen creating something by your side fulfilled a part of me I didn't know was missing. That you were, are, and always will be the man I compare to all others."

His insides swished and swirled with an excitement that made him feel alive and ready to take on the world. "I need to call my ex-wife more often if it triggers this kind of response."

She swatted at him. "That's what you say to woman who poured her heart out to you? Damon Reynolds, you're a scoundrel." She bolted up from the chair, but he was there, in her space, and never intended to let her go again.

"I'm a scoundrel who's been in love with you from the

159

Ciara Knight

time he started to drive." He couldn't hold back another second and kissed her hard, passionately, and with all the love he'd been holding back for decades.

When Badger barked and they were left heaving and clinging to each other as if in fear the other would slip away, he whispered, "After all this time, I finally have you, and nothing will tear us apart again. You can go do any show you want, you can go on tour, I don't care. I'll visit you in every city. I'll follow you across the world, and I'll always remain here at my restaurant waiting for you to come home."

"No need. I'm not going anywhere. It's time for a new chapter of my life. I spoke to Bri, and she put me in touch with her agent, who wants to see my scripts. I'm staying and I'm going to write, but I might need a job. You looking for a cook? Well, a cook in training?"

"You're welcome in my kitchen anytime." He couldn't help but realize it had taken him over fifty years, but he'd finally found his life balance and happiness.

Chapter Twenty

WIND CLAPPED THEN TURNED to her makeshift practice audience in the restaurant, consisting of her Friendsters, Rhonda, and a few board members.

Applause echoed through the space full of eclectic Mediterranean art and painted tables and chairs in vibrant colors mixed with copper fixtures and even a stone wall. Damon had gone all out.

"Marvelous," Mrs. Sheffield said.

Rhonda shot from the chair, tipping it backward with a bang. Joey covered his ears and ran to Mannie's side while humming. "That's not my play. What happened to my script?"

Wind plastered on a placating smile. "I made a few modifications, that's all. You know, to fit the actors and their gifts. That's what this is all about, right? Helping these amazing children?"

"Modifications? There's nothing in there I wrote."

Rhonda crossed her arms over her chest. "Take my name off the program. I didn't co-write this simple garble." She raised her chin. "There isn't any complexity or symbolism in this story. It's just...just...a tale of some kids and a dog." She bolted out the door, and Wind held her breath then looked to Kat.

Mrs. Sheffield snagged her purse from the seat, sending Wind's pulse into a percussion line of beats. "Well, I, for one, am glad that Wind took over the script writing and now I have Rhonda off our backs."

"I swear, I tried to rewrite her manuscript, but I couldn't. I had to start from scratch. What will this mean for the restaurant's final inspection? I thought there was some deal made with Skipper."

"Yes, and we fulfilled it." Mrs. Sheffield puffed her hair and headed for the door. "I didn't fire her. She quit. Not my problem now or yours. Children, amazing job. This is good enough to be on a Broadway stage."

Wind gave Sarah Jane two thumbs-up. She smiled brightly and reciprocated, her pigtail sprouts bouncing like pom-poms on her head.

Kat turned from the iron and bronze doors and then moved to the table near Wind. "You should be proud of yourself."

"No. It's the children who should be proud. They've come such a long way."

"I can't believe they're doing this. I mean, Joey's up on a stage in front of people and even looked at the audience once." Kat dabbed at her eyes. Apparently, the post-pregnancy hormones were still lurking around.

"I always knew they could do it."

"Yes, you did." Kat squeezed her forearm. "Girl, you are such a gift to this world. Don't ever let anyone tell you differently."

"She is a special gift to us all." Damon slipped his arm around her waist from behind.

"Thanks for allowing us to practice here today. There was a scheduling conflict with the Shack, and we still can't house anything at the center until we finish jumping through a few more political hoops."

"Speaking of. I spoke to Angela, and she's looking into who caused the grant money to be reappropriated." He squeezed Wind a little tighter against him. "I still think you should have more than one grant, but Wind explained it was a way to get the place up and going and you will be trying to get more grant money moving forward."

"Yes, well, I wish we had more now." Kat sighed, and Damon slipped away as fast as he'd appeared. "You two look awfully happy together. I knew he'd see you for the real bright star you are." She glanced at her watch. "We can talk more about that when I meet you at Friendship Beach for our sunset girls' hour." She headed through the door with a shout. "Don't be late this time."

Wind ignored her because everyone knew she'd be late. That's why they probably gave her a time thirty minutes before they were all actually planning on being there. She moved the few chairs they'd claimed as audience seats back into place while Sarah Jane put away the props and Joey sat next to Mannie, both petting Badger in the corner.

"This here's my favorite animal." He raised his cane at Wind. "Don't go telling Houdini that. He's no ordinary animal, so he's still my favorite mischievous matchmaker."

Joey scratched Badger's head and smiled up at Mannie. Wind wanted to run over and give them both a hug. The boy responded to speech and even interacted with Mannie now, even if non-verbally.

A whisk against metal drew Wind's attention to the kitchen. "What's going on back there?"

"Trying some variations to my chocolate lava mini-cakes for the show."

She nudged the door open and sniffed the most amazing chocolatey goodness. "*Mmm*, that smells so good."

"Come taste it." Damon lifted a spoon with deep-brown liquid oozing over the sides and dripping into the bowl.

She opened her mouth and savored the richness. "Wow."

He kissed then nibbled the edge of her lips. "Yes, it is."

The parents arrived, pulling Wind away from Damon, but she couldn't wait to return. Once everyone left, she knew she needed to get back to Jewels's to change and make it to Trevor's dock to take the dinghy before Jewels left, or she'd be paddling it across the river to their private Friendster Beach. "Meet me tonight so we can comb through all the options and try to fix this mess."

Damon set one of the fluffy, chocolaty mounds of goodness on a cooling rack, took her by the hand, and spun her around and then into his arms. "I'm not sure I can make it a few hours, but I'll do my best."

"Good thing we're both here to stay, then." A warning nibbled at her. "Hear back from Angela yet?"

"No, but I'm sure she'll call me this afternoon or Serena will." He kissed her cheek. "Don't worry. I told you she said there was no price to pay."

Wind pushed from his arms and grabbed her purse. "Don't be so naive. If she's as manipulative as you said she was, then there will be a price to pay. Trust me. Just make sure you're prepared to stand your ground."

"I'll channel my inner Wind. Don't worry. She has no hold over me anymore. I owe her nothing, and nothing could tear me away from this town, my restaurant, and you." He winked and strutted across the restaurant with that hungry gaze of his.

Wind held her hand up. "No, you stay five feet away. I can't be late again. Besides, I've always left my fans wanting more."

"Then I want a lot because I'm your biggest fan."

She hurried out the door and raced to Jewels's to get ready to head out to Friendship Beach. Because the quicker she got to the girls' hour, the quicker she could return to Damon and their plan to save the center's funding. Together.

Chapter Twenty-One

Damon swept up the last of the cracker remanent. *Mental note: Joey doesn't eat anything brown or orange, Paul has a peanut allergy, and Mannie can only eat soft food. And he likes to complain.*

He dumped the last of the appetizers he'd made since his waistline didn't need it and thought about taking a run on the beach. It was a waiting game until opening now.

With the last bit of crumbs in his dustpan, he stood and looked around the room. Finished. Everything he'd imagined had come to fruition.

"So you finally did it. The place you always talked about." Serena's voice echoed from behind him.

He spun around, and his heart soared at the sight of his daughter. He abandoned the broom and dustpan in favor of holding his only daughter. "My baby girl."

He swooped her into his arms and spun her around.

"Dad, I'm not a little girl anymore."

"Right, sorry." He put her down on her three-inch heels and took a step back. Her highlighted blonde hair was perfectly ironed out in a straight shine, her suit was cut to perfection, and her complexion was flawless, but even through the makeup, he could see the dark circles. "She's been working you too hard."

"Don't start. Again, grown woman here. And Mom doesn't expect any more out of me than any of her other staff."

"As I said, she's working you too hard."

She set her oversized purse on the table and patted his shoulder. "I knew you missed us." With a twirl and a smile, she faced him. "You did it. Finally, you've recreated that place we ate at in the Mediterranean."

He blinked and thought back but couldn't find the memory.

"The one from when Mom got stuck back in some winter storm in New York and you and I spent the weekend on the island. We ate at this place every afternoon. It's the highlight of my childhood. We had this magical two days of nothing but sun, fun, and bonding. Now it's here."

The memories of that weekend flooded in on him. "I hadn't realized it, but yes. This place does remind me of that little spot on the beach. We stayed next door to it in that tiny apartment. I thought you'd find it disgusting and below your standards, especially sharing a room with your old man, but we spent evenings gossiping and watching old movies and days playing games on the deck of the restaurant and swimming in the ocean."

"Like it? Dad, this *is* the place." She ran a finger along the yellow-painted table. "Now that you've opened it here, you should open one in New York. It'll be a huge hit. I can help with—"

"I'm happy here."

"Dad, come on. This was a pause. You don't belong in this little town. Sure, it's great to take a vacation, but you're still too young to go shrivel away in Bluehairville."

"That's not insulting at all. Better be careful flinging those kinds of terms around since your mother is running on some sort of feel-good platform." His temper sparked. "Let me be clear. I'm happy here. I've made amazing friends."

"Friends? Ha." She crossed her arms over her chest. "I hope you're being careful. If the media catches on that you're involved with another woman during Mom's campaign, you'll be swarming with reporters here. You'll be back in the middle of the madness in an instant."

"We're divorced, and my life is finally my own." He let out an exhausted sigh. "Listen, I don't want to ever say anything negative about your mother. I want you to have a relationship with us both, but I won't be dragged into her world again. So tell me now, did she call and send you here to convince me to do something for her? If she wants me to stop seeing Wind, she can forget it. I'm my own man now."

She raised a brow at him. "Wind?"

"Yes, and you can report back that I'm happy and if

any reporter shows up here, I'll say what I've been instructed to say and what I've said every time I've been asked. 'We're still best of friends. Angela was a loving and caring wife and is an excellent mother, but we married young and we realized we were better as friends, but we still support each other. And I for one will be voting for her in the next election.'"

"Don't sound so rehearsed. And Mom didn't send me. I haven't spoken to her in a couple of weeks. We've been in two different time zones, and we're gearing up to announce her run for the presidential primaries. Can you imagine Mom as president?" Her eyes glowed with admiration.

"Yes. I've always thought she'd achieve all her political aspirations." Angela's words erupted in his mind. "Wait, she said you were the one who told her about the center for special needs."

"What?" A flash of confusion told him everything he needed to know. She straightened. "Oh, right. I left her a message about it."

He straightened and approached his daughter. "I raised you better than to lie, but apparently covering for your mother now merits you lying to your father."

"Dad, I'm not—"

"Don't. As much as you want to be like your mother, you're not able to pull off the blank affect and distant emotions. That's a compliment, not an insult."

"Stop. Mom isn't that bad. And I could do worse for a role model."

"Me?" Every muscle in his body stiffened. His anger boiled over and fell into disappointment. "I see."

"Dad, I didn't mean..."

"Right." He needed some air. This wasn't how he'd hoped his first reunion with his little girl would go. The way she looked at him said it all. "You think I came here because your mother broke me after the divorce, but you have it all wrong. I'm finally pieced back together into the life I've always wanted. Now, if you'll excuse me, I'm going for a run on the beach. I hope you're here when I return. If so, I'll make us a nice dinner, and you can be the first person to dine in my new restaurant."

"Dad." She chased after him, but he didn't stop.

"I'll be back soon. Feel free to go up the street to the hotel and tell Dustin that you need a room."

"I'm only here for the day," she called after him, but he didn't stop because in his emotional state, he'd say something he'd regret and he'd always held his temper with his children.

After a long run on the beach, shower, and shave, he returned to the restaurant in hopes his daughter remained. He opened the door, but didn't see his baby girl. Instead, he saw Angela standing in the middle of his world.

Chapter Twenty Two

THE DINGHY BOUNCED along the wake of a passing boat, despite the "no wake" zone. A few choice words erupted from Trace's mouth. Apparently, some things didn't change. But finally, Wind had realized why the women she'd been friends with on and off for almost their entire lives had been changed by love. Now that she and Damon... She startled. Was she? In love? Infatuation, yes. But she'd never thrown around the big L word.

"Wind Lively has been tamed by a man," Kat said in a teasing tone.

"I'm untamable." She held her fingers in the water spitting up from the ocean around their little craft. The cool, flittering touch of water felt more refreshing than normal.

Jewels adjusted herself on the siderail of the dinghy. "I wouldn't say you were tamed. Blinded and lovesick maybe."

Wind teasingly pushed Jewels, but not hard enough to really send her overboard.

Trace laughed. "I'd say she's whipped."

"Alright, stop. I'm still me, and I can out sass all of you."

"We'll stop after you tell us why you're so anxious to leave our girl power hour. Where are you off to?"

She eyed the dock ahead. "It's not what you think."

"Going to see Damon, huh?" Trace said in a twelve-year-old-crush voice.

"Not for the reasons you think."

"Too bad. I was thinking hot and dishonorable." Jewels winked.

Wind shook her head. "You're one to talk, girl. You best get married before the town discovers your scandalous all-nighters."

"All night? Ohhhh. You better put a ring on it, girl." Trace held up her own sparkling diamond, and Kat followed suit.

Wind looked down at her own hand. Could she imagine a ring ever residing on her left hand?

"Not about me at the moment. We were focusing on Wind's hot date." Jewels pointed at her while still holding on to the rope handle with the other hand.

"Fine, yes, I'm going to see him, but not for the reasons you think. We're going to look through grants and dig deeper into funding. We're going to band together and try to figure out how to help."

Kat's eyes dimmed. "I appreciate the help. We're still digging, and Wes has some calls out. Unfortunately, his connections are more in the tech field than politics."

"Don't worry. I think, together, Damon and I will figure something out."

Trace docked the dinghy, and Kat hopped out to tie it to the cleat. "All night, huh?"

Wind crawled out and bolted from her inquisitive friends and the bouncing, spine-jolting boat. "Ta-ta for now, ladies. I've got work to do."

"Don't work all night," Jewels called out.

"Goodbye, town harlot."

Wind gave a backhand wave and escaped from her loving and sometimes overbearing friends. But she wouldn't want it any other way.

She hiked up the small hill onto the asphalt road next to the hotel. All afternoon she'd been distracted, not only because of Damon but because she had a clue about what she wanted to do with her life next. It sounded insane. Too insane to even share with her girls, but if anyone understood insane dreams and wanting to work hard to get them, it would be Damon. Would he support her even if it meant she'd have to travel to New York often? He'd said he'd deal with it.

Of course, it wouldn't be as much as if she'd gone back to acting, and what she wanted probably would never happen. It had never been done before, but she'd challenged bigger odds than a Broadway play with a special needs cast. She pulled in talent from all over the country. Based on what those kids had done with no training in their little town, she could really bring light to the differences of people through art.

Her heart pumped faster and her steps felt lighter. She threw open the door to the restaurant without a thought, but didn't see Damon. She did hear voices. Badger sat obediently near the kitchen with a snarl on his face.

She squatted down, her nerves firing, the hair on her arms standing straight. Voices, female, wafted from the kitchen.

"If you want to save that center, then you'll abandon this insanity and return to New York with me. I'll help you open a restaurant. In exchange, you'll stand by my side and tell everyone I was a good wife and you want to reconcile until I reach the White House."

Wind froze, every muscle tightening in warning. No, he wouldn't fall into that world again, would he?

"I told you before that I'm not interested in your world anymore, and I can't believe you sent Serena here to guilt me into helping you."

"I didn't. She was worried and wanted to check on you."

Wind started breathing again. Good, he was sticking up for himself, not allowing his ex to guilt him into her life anymore.

"New York restaurant, huh?"

Wait, was that interest in his voice? It couldn't be. He

liked it here. No, he loved it. Loved her. Not that he said those exact words, but it was understood.

"And that hussy. You've got to end that. How would it look if you were involved with some entertainer when you want to reunite with me? That's not good for our image."

"Don't pull her into this." Steps sounded back and forth on the kitchen floor. "You swear that this is it. The last time you pull me into this world. That I'll keep this restaurant and return here someday."

"No!" Wind shot up and shoved open the door to the kitchen. "Don't do this."

A woman standing in a perfectly designed, hip-hugging suit with her hair up in an old-fashioned French twist eyed her up and down. Her younger twin, but with her hair pulled back at the nape of her neck, glowered at Wind.

"Wind. You don't understand." Damon rushed to her side and took her hands, but she yanked them away.

Her gaze darted between his ex, his daughter, and him. "We were going to figure this out together. You were done with your manipulating ex. We had plans."

"Please, give me a chance to explain."

Angela strolled over. "What's to explain? You're sacrificing your dreams to save the day. Predictable as always."

Wind backstepped away, putting distance between her heart and the empty promises of a shell of a man she thought had become the man of her dreams.

"It's the only way to save the program, your play, all of you, and those children. I can't let all of you down."

"But you're letting yourself down. I thought you trusted us. Trusted that we would figure this out together. Instead, you're martyring yourself again. I guess I was right. You're nothing like your father. You're worse."

She spun on her heels and raced from the restaurant, from the man she thought she knew and loved, from her happily ever after.

Rain drizzled down from the night sky, but she didn't care. She raced down the street, the hill, the beach, and didn't stop until she reached Jewels's place. She flung open the door, mascara running down her face, hair plastered down by water.

The girls jumped from their perspective positions and surrounded her.

"What happened? Who do we have to kill?"

She wanted to laugh at Trace's words, but she couldn't, only tears streaked down her face. "I'm a fool. I trusted him. He's still the self-righteous, spineless man I knew all those years ago. At least I got one thing out of this. I can finally let go of my childish fantasy of the perfect man that got away, because this time I'm throwing him out of my life."

"Girl, I'm so sorry." Jewels hugged her tight.

Trace left the room and returned with a towel. "Where is he? Kat, you can help bury the body, right?"

"Absolutely." Kat took the towel and dabbed at Wind's face. "As much as I want you to stay, I'll take you to the airport myself if that's what you want. After we run him out of town, you can come back for a visit."

As broken as her heart was, those kids needed her. "No, I'm not going anywhere. In fact, I have a plan, and I'm going to get to work on the next act of my life. I know what I want to do now. If you'll excuse me, I have some emails to send and a play to write."

Chapter Twenty-Three

Damon ran all the way to Jewels's place. Rain pelted his thin T-shirt. Lightning chained from cloud to ominous cloud. Despite the hour, he pounded on the door, but no one answered. "Wind, listen to me. I need to explain."

He swiped the water dripping from his hair into his eyes. His body shook from cold, from fear, from loss. He wasn't sure. But the more he knocked, the more he shivered.

No sounds, no lights.

He pounded again and again. Houdini popped his head out of the curtains and chattered at him through the window.

"Listen, it's okay. It was a bluff. I didn't really cave or play the part of a martyr." He pressed his palm to the glass window, willing Houdini to take his side and go chastise Wind for not coming out. "Great. I'm talking to a rodent."

Houdini chittered at him one last time and then disappeared into the darkness.

Car lights beamed in from the road, but he didn't care. He pounded on the door again. "Wind, I'm not leaving. I'm not trying to drive you away. I've grown and am a wiser man. I know I broke up with you all those years ago so that I could set you free to pursue your dreams. I thought I was doing the right thing."

"Come on, man. Time for you to go." Dustin's voice echoed through the small front courtyard between the old, abandoned souvenir shop and his hollow heart.

"No, you don't understand. Wind overheard something, but she didn't know why I said those things." He pounded once more, and Dustin and Trevor moved in closer. "Seriously? I thought we were friends. I thought I was an honorary Manster."

"That's why we're here. Wind wanted to call the police. Time to go."

Agitation wormed its way into his plea. "The police? Really? Apparently, you haven't changed. Instead of coming out here and facing me, you want to do the dramatic thing?" Anger bubbled to the surface. "You were so quick to judge. You didn't even give me a chance to explain. You assumed the worst."

Dustin touched his shoulder, but he shrugged him away. "I guess I know how much my word means now. How much you trust me. What you truly think of me. How could you compare me to my father?" His voice cracked. "I thought you were the one person who understood. Understood why I stood by my wife all those years. Understood now why I wanted this life so badly. Understood how much I wanted to be with you."

His emotions raged war, thundering through him more than the storm brewed around them. Florida at its best. A dark and stormy night for the end of a dark and stormy relationship.

He threw his hands up in the air and stepped away from the front porch, eyeing both the men who stood by, ready to force him from Jewels's house if that's what it took. Part of him wanted to fight. To punch something, anything. Apparently, he *wasn't* that different from his father.

The realization took the fight from him, trickling into the gutter with the rainwater. "You know, I trusted you. I thought you were going to be my person. But I guess that position's already been filled by the Friendsters. I should've known there was no room left for me. Go back to Broadway, Wind. I'll figure out how to beat my ex and save the center, but what I won't do is sell my restaurant and leave, so if you don't want to see me every day, you should go."

He walked away. Away from the woman he thought knew him best and loved him anyway.

WIND RESTED her forehead against the door, tears streaming down her face.

Jewels rubbed small circles on her back. "Tell me to go if you want, but I think you should hear him out."

"But I heard him with my own ears," Wind argued more with herself than with Jewels.

"I know you. You'll never be happy unless you have the final word. You gonna let him get away with saying his piece without your response? That's not the Wind Lively I know."

She chuckled and shook her head. "You're right about one thing. Wind Lively always has the last word." She straightened her polka dot pajama top and lifted her chin.

Jewels opened the door, and Wind spotted Damon's back. "That's it?"

He turned, his face muted in the darkness, so she stepped out into the storm and faced him. "Thought you pounded on my door to explain." She stepped out into the cold, irritatingly piercing raindrops and stood in the center of the courtyard. "So, tell me."

He looked to the men as if to get permission to stay but didn't wait for a reply before he took a step into the courtyard. "I told Angela what I needed to so that she wouldn't know what I was really up to. I came up with a plan, but I couldn't execute it if she knew what it was. She has too many friends and could cut another deal. I realized the moment I saw her in my kitchen and she slipped about finding out about the center from my daughter that it was her who did this. She blocked that grant."

"So you thought it was your fault so you'd fix everything, even if it meant giving up your life here."

He bolted toward her, but she took a step back, knowing one touch would make her forget her concerns. If he gave into his ex-wife today, he'd give into her again in the future. A future she'd dreamed of sharing with him.

"No. I lied so that I could have time to get your help. All of your help." He gestured to Jewels's house, then back to the men, and then to her. "I've got an idea, but I can't do it alone. It will take perfect timing, and I'll need Wes and Kat to be on board, not to mention getting the legal paperwork drawn up."

She shuffled a half step toward him. "What plan?" Her hair fell over her eyes in a clumpy, awful mess, but she didn't care. For once in her life, she didn't care if she was the most stunning one in the room.

"A plan that involves not only her approval of grant money but also the money from an opposing political party. A bipartisan moment, where you, Wind, will make sure the media shows to capture a historic moment where both parties come together to fix a problem beyond their governmental excuses of insurance issues. They will come together to offer a new and innovative solution to help our children with special needs in this country."

The plan unfolded in her brain. "And since it'll be captured for all to see, Angela won't be able to back out, even when she discovers you're staying here and not going to New York."

"I knew you were smart." He winked, pushing his hair from his eyes.

That's when she noticed he wasn't a martyr or a weak

man. He was a smart man who looked sexier than an underwear model, had the voice of James Earl Jones and the sexual chemistry of Burt Lancaster, and she was Deborah Kerr, and the courtyard was their beach.

He took a step toward her, but she couldn't give in to her desire, not yet. "I might be going to Broadway."

He stopped. "I told you I supported whatever your dreams in the future were. Go back to performing. It won't change anything."

His words were honest, but his voice sounded as if his heart ached.

"No, not to perform. I want to start a production that only has a cast of characters with special needs. A show that will show people their true gifts."

He smiled—a true, proud, I-want-you-even-more grin. "I'll help any way I can. I think that's an amazing new career path for you. But I just have one question."

"What's that?"

He took another step. "Can I visit you when you're not too busy?"

"No."

He stopped.

She smiled. "Because I won't be moving there. I'll be writing the play and will travel up there for casting, but I'm going to get a director friend of mine to help. Yes, I'll have to travel up there, but my home base will be here."

His eyes lit up with hope and passion and want. "I love you, Wind Lively."

"I know." She flew into his arms.

He cupped her cheeks and studied her face as if to remember every feature. Then his lips claimed hers, and she was lost in a whirl of wind and rain, and she didn't care. All she cared about was never letting go of the man who made her feel alive and young and complete.

Chapter Twenty Four

Wind corralled Joey, Sarah Jane, Paul, and the rest of the children to their side of the front entry.

Angela leaned in and said, "Can't you control them? I need them to look good for the photo op."

Damon headed her way, but Wind shot him a warning glare. She knew it had been difficult for him to hold his tongue the first five times she'd slung insults at Wind since she'd arrived to wait for the press. Good thing Wind could act, because it was taking all her skills to act humble and upset about her stealing Damon from her. "I'm doing my best."

"Your best isn't good enough. If you can't control them, then keep the one in the wheelchair and send the rest home. He'll be the best for the photos."

Wind ground her teeth. It was one thing to insult her but another thing to insult the children. But she was just giving Wind more material to use for her villain in her new Broadway play, *Can You See Me?*

The last media truck pulled up, and Serena waved them all to take their places. The last cameraman set up, and they all took their spots.

Damon held up a hand. "Wait. We're missing something—well, someone."

Angela shot him a sideways, narrowed-eyed warning but then softened and smiled at the cameras. A black SUV pulled up, and out stepped Ronald Bowling with his entourage of lackeys.

"What's going on? What's he doing here?"

Wind stepped forward to take center stage. "Senator Bowling, we're so thankful you've taken time out of your busy schedule to be here today. This is a historic moment. Damon, would you like to deliver a speech?"

Kat and Wes finished speaking with Channel Two and joined them, smiling from ear to ear. Dustin, Trace, Jewels, and Trevor stood on the outskirts of the commotion, ready to help out with any of the kids if needed.

Damon joined her. "I'd be happy to." He kissed Wind's cheek and took her by the hand. A gasp sounded from Angela, but by the time they took their places with the large scissors in hand at the red ribbon, she'd already recovered. "It is our great pleasure to announce that despite opposing political views, these two senators have come together, putting aside their own political agendas to help our children."

Hands rose, cameras snapped, and video cameras moved in.

Damon cleared his throat and glanced at both senators. "This center is a new way of bringing back the trust of the American people by providing services insurance doesn't cover for our lost and forgotten. A new way of combating the systemic problem of inadequate services for our children due to financial issues the hardworking people of this country are burdened with. Thanks to Senator Angela Reynolds, whose heroic actions fixed a situation where our government considered revoking our grant to designate funds for another purpose, and Senator Bowling, who saved the day by matching the grant money so that now we can open with no fear of shutting down due to lack of funds in the near future."

He paused, and Wind stepped forward to take it home, but Damon continued. "As a matter of fact, they have even agreed to lend their support for a new Broadway production, *Can You See Me?*. This show will be the first of its kind to showcase the gifts of children and adults with unique challenges. The script for this musical was written by the amazingly talented Broadway veteran Wind Lively."

He kissed her hand and then looked directly at the camera. "And the woman I love."

Cameras and questions erupted, which apparently sparked Angela's and Senator Bowling's attention, because they took center stage to answer questions while Damon ushered Wind away as Kat and Wes did the official ribbon cutting.

"That was such a rush," Damon said, cuddling Wind into him at the side of the building.

"Yes, it was. Now we have a dinner and play to pull off. We better get back to the restaurant." Wind tugged at him, but he held her tight.

"But I want to spend more time with you."

"After tonight, we can spend all the time we want together. I'm thinking a midnight swim and cuddling on the beach watching the stars."

He nuzzled her ear. "Sounds perfect."

Before she lost herself in Damon, she rushed him to the restaurant, and they worked hard to prep dinner. The kids arrived, and Mannie took the stage and helped them take their spots.

News crews snuck in, but she instructed them to remain in the back and not distract the children or it could ruin their concentration. To her surprise, the few reporters who'd remained behaved exactly as instructed.

The crowd sat silently, and Wind's nerves fluttered inside. To her delight, Joey, Badger, Mannie, Sarah Jane, Paul, and all the others performed exactly how they'd practiced it. Damon, Bri, and her stepdaughter stood by ready to clear plates but not interfere during the production.

At the final scene, Wind held her breath. Joey stood and accepted Badger's leash. Mannie said his line, and Joey faced the audience and said, "I will."

His father clapped but stopped himself when Joey

cringed. His mother sat swiping at her tears. Joey looked up at Wind and gave two thumbs-up. She reciprocated, and tears rolled down her own cheeks.

Damon came over and hugged her into his side. "You did that."

"No, Joey did that. I'm so proud of him." Wind watched the children take their final bows and then helped clear the tables, but she kept getting pulled away by a reporter asking about her plans for Broadway and if Joey would be a part of it.

By the end of the night, she collapsed into a chair with hope in her heart and sore toes on her feet, surrounded by all her friends. Damon came out, along with Jewels, and they placed a chocolate lava cake in front of each couple and an extra for Tabitha.

Jewels and Damon kept glancing at each other.

"What is it?" Wind was starved, so she didn't wait for their answer before picking up her fork and diving into the lava cake, hitting something solid. "Ah, what's that?"

Trevor did the same thing. "Is there a buried treasure in these treats, or did someone drop some nails into the mix?"

"Nothing in mine," Wes announced.

Wind pulled out something with her fork and wiped it clean. A ring. She shot a glance at Trevor, who held up a gold band. Her heart skittered and skipped, flipped and flew. "Ah, what's going on?"

Damon got down on one knee, as did Jewels. "We wanted to do something memorable. I thought all of our friends would want to share in this moment, so I hope you will say yes so I don't look like a fool, because Wind, you make me feel alive and free and I love you more than I can express with words."

Jewels sniffled. "I know I've been fighting this for a long time, but I know now that I want to spend the rest of my days with you. If you'll have me, I hope we can spend the rest of our time together keeping our spark alive."

Trevor scooped her into his arms. "I certainly want to try."

Wind was so mesmerized by her dear friend finally accepting a new love in her life that she didn't realize she hadn't given her own answer.

Kat nudged her. "Uh, don't leave the man hanging."

"Yes. A thousand times yes." Wind held up her left hand and kissed him. "I love you so much. I say we get married before your ex comes up with a plan to stop us."

"Don't have to worry about that. I can handle her."

"Yes, you can." Wind winked and glanced at their little stage at the end of the restaurant.

Trace threw her hands up. "No. You can't..."

Damon's brows rose. "Why can't we get married soon?"

"You can get married now, but I see what Wind's thinking. You can't do it, or we'll never live it down."

"I'm not following." Damon looked between them.

Kat laughed. "Jewels knows things before they happen, and before I married Wes, she told Jewels she knew where she'd get married. We all assumed it would be some big production, but Jewels said no, it would be on a small stage somewhere quiet."

Jewels laughed. "I'm not one to say I told you so, but..."

"You did. And I'm glad your prediction came true." Wind took Damon by the hand. "All I have or want for the wedding is in this room. What do you say?"

"I say it's time to build a home because it's going to get awfully crowded at Jewels's place."

"Actually, you can move into the old souvenir shop until your place is ready. Dustin and Trevor converted it to an apartment for Wind in case she stayed."

"How'd you manage to do that without me knowing?" Wind asked.

Dustin and Trevor laughed. "You've both been distracted. It wasn't difficult."

When darkness fell, Damon lit the tiki torches, and they all relaxed on the back deck, looking up at the stars and listening to the waves crash onto the shore.

Wind snuggled into Damon's side and whispered, "Who knew a new life could begin at fifty?"

Damon nibbled her ear. "I think because we already lived the life we thought we were supposed to, but now we get to live the one we want. And I want to live the rest of my life here, in this town, with our friends, loving you."

The End

Recipe

Cherry Mimosa
    Ingredients:

- 7 ounces seedless cherries
- 1 bottle (750 ml) Prosecco or for non-alcoholic option use seltzer or sparkling water
- 1 and 1/2 cups fresh orange juice

Instructions:
Place cherries and 1 cup orange juice into a blender and blend until smooth. Divide cherry mixture among serving glasses, then top with remaining 1/2 cup (125ml) orange juice and prosecco.
Serve immediately.

Reader's Guide

1. One of my editors mentioned that it was nice to see the softer side of Wind in her own story. Did you feel like you've seen a new side to Wind Lively?

2. Do you think Wind tried too hard in the beginning to prove herself to Damon? If so, why?

3. How do you think Wind felt facing the end of a career she'd worked so hard to earn for so many years?

4. Why do you think Damon's first marriage didn't work out? Do you think he should have done more to save it? If so, how?

5. Why do you think Wind wanted to remain in Summer Island? Is it only because of Damon or do you think being a godmother, a friend, and having her town family around her

influenced her decision? Do you think she would've remained in Summer Island if things didn't work out with Damon?

6. Do you think Damon fits in well with the Mansters?

7. Why do you think Jewels hesitated so long to marry Trevor?

8. What has been your favorite story in the Friendship Beach series?

9. Do you think Damon and Wind will live happily ever after?

10. Do you want another season of the Friendship Beach series? If so, make sure to let Ciara Knight know by filling out her contact form on ciaraknight.com. She answers all messages personally.

Also by Ciara Knight

For a complete list of my books, please visit my website at www. ciaraknight.com. A great way to keep up to date on all releases, sales and prizes subscribe to my Newsletter. I'm extremely sociable, so feel free to chat with me on Facebook, Twitter, or Goodreads.

For your convenience please see my complete title list below, in reading order:

CONTEMPORARY ROMANCE

Friendship Beach Series

Summer Island Book Club

Summer Island Sisters

Summer Island Hope

Summer Island Romance

Sweetwater County Series

Winter in Sweetwater County

Spring in Sweetwater County

Summer in Sweetwater County

Fall in Sweetwater County

Christmas in Sweetwater County

Valentines in Sweet-water County

Fourth of July in Sweetwater County

Thanksgiving in Sweetwater County

Grace in Sweetwater County

Faith in Sweetwater County

Love in Sweetwater County

A Sugar Maple Holiday Novel

(Historical)

If You Keep Me

If You Choose Me

A Sugar Maple Novel

If You Love Me

If You Adore Me

If You Cherish Me

If You Hold Me

If You Kiss Me

Riverbend

In All My Wishes

In All My Years

In All My Dreams

In All My Life

A Christmas Spark

A Miracle Mountain Christmas

HISTORICAL WESTERNS:

McKinnie Mail Order Brides Series

Love on the Prairie

(USA Today Bestselling Novel)

Love in the Rockies

Love on the Plains

Love on the Ranch

His Holiday Promise

(A Love on the Ranch Novella)

Love on the Sound

Love on the Border

Love at the Coast

A Prospectors Novel

Fools Rush

Bride of America

Adelaide: Bride of Maryland

About the Author

Ciara Knight is a USA TODAY Bestselling Author, who writes clean and wholesome romance novels set in either modern day small towns or wild historic old west. Born with a huge imagination that usually got her into trouble, Ciara is happy she's found a way to use her powers for good. She loves spending time with her characters and hopes you do, too.

Made in the USA
Columbia, SC
12 October 2022